Why Him?

A Second Natasha McMorales Mystery

C S Thompson

Why Him?

Published in the U.S. by:

CSThompsonBooks.com
Bristol, TN 37620

Copyright © 2011 by Chuck Thompson. All rights reserved.

ISBN 978-0-9794116-5-6

This is a work of fiction. Names, characters, events and incidents are either the products of the author's imagination or used in a fictitious manner. Any resemblance to actual persons, living or dead, or actual events is purely coincidental.

Although the major characters are all fictional and any resemblance to a real person is accidental and unintentional, many of the places are real and the people one would find there are real as well. Those places include:

In the Bristol Area: Blackbird Bakery, Eatz on 5th, Ellis' of Abingdon, King College, Manna Bagel, Session 27, & State Street

In the Asheville, NC area: The Grove Park Inn, Malaprops, Renaissance Hotel, Salsas, Sweet Mommas, Tupelo Honey Café, & World Market

In the Washington DC area: Chinatown, Legal Seafood, Lincoln Memorial, National Mall, National Museum of the American Indian, Smithsonian Air & Space Museum, and the Washington Monument

(Nattie's review of *Murder Takes the Cake* can be seen at her blog, nattiemoreland.blogspot.com, on the 16th of August 2010)

Special thanks to:

Everyone who has read *Why Natasha?* or is friends with her on Facebook

Craig McDonald for editing, encouragement, and the impetus idea from which the plot sprang.

Sarah Barker for reading and constructive suggestions.

Tommy Bryant for insisting on more danger

Karen Rohr and JB Madison for reading.

Erin Reardon for promotion ideas and encouragement

Paige Morgan & Pua Coffman for guest appearances in Chapter 20

And finally, Barb Thompson for making my life work

PROLOGUE

"The last six months have been quite a ride," he said to no one in particular. No one heard him anyway. The couple in the corner was so engrossed in each other that they would not have heard him if he had been sitting at their table. And the bartender, a huge man with a receding hairline, a well trimmed beard, and his thinning hair pulled back into a tight ponytail was cleaning up at the other end of the bar where an attractive young blond woman with her own ponytail sat looking at her watch every few minutes.

After an admiring inspection of the blond, who looked like she could have been a Hooters model, he looked at himself in the mirror across from the bar and smiled. It had been a long time. Six months ago his career was going nowhere, and his wife was in her own world. And now he had the Midas touch.

The head of his department, a pompous bureaucrat who never gave him the time of day, now treated him like the golden boy. Money had not started rolling in, but it was going to, and soon. His worries would soon be over. He was more relaxed, more energized, and happier; and if his wife was a good judge of it, he was even funnier.

"To us." He hoisted the mug to his reflection in the mirror and then took a long drink.

"Are you ready for another one?" asked the bartender with a slight Cajun accent not usually found in Northeast Tennessee.

He looked at the other end of the bar where the bartender had been. The blonde's date had arrived and sat down next to her. He was not as big as the bartender but he was quite large himself. The tight tee shirt gave testimony to many hours spent in the weight room. And the face above the tight tee shirt did not look like it would understand a bartender's attention given "innocently" to his girlfriend.

"I'm good, but thanks." He nodded towards the blonde. "Pretty girl."

"Oh really?" The bartender yawned and glanced in the direction of the blonde. He tipped his head to the right for as moment, and then to the left as he looked at her, "I hadn't noticed."

He smiled.

"Is your friend coming back?" asked the bartender.

He looked at the empty seat next to him. His friend, as the bartender called him, had left fifteen minutes ago.

"No, he's not coming back, and I must hit the road now, too."

He laid a ten-dollar bill on the bar and headed for the exit. The blonde's date scowled at him as he walked by. He was tempted to wink at the big guy, but decided just to nod.

He stood for a moment on the edge of the gravel parking lot enjoying the crispness of the night air. The faint smell of a wood fire in the distance inspired him to breathe even more deeply. He walked slowly to his car, enjoying the crunching sound the gravel made under his feet and the night smells.

As he slid his key into the door of his Honda Civic, he was startled by the sounds of someone running across the gravel. Wanting to look in the direction of the noise he tried to remove the key from the door, but it was stuck. Frustration at the sticky key made him forget the sound momentarily as he thought that tolerating little nuisances like having to jiggle a car key to get it to work would be part of his past as soon as the money started to come his way.

He was jolted from his daydream as the sound of the footsteps got closer and closer behind him. Frustration with his car returned, which made him fumble even more trying to remove his key. Finally, either by strength or by panic, he was able to rip the keys free. His shoulders tightened involuntarily as he turned to face whoever it was that was rushing towards him.

"You!" he exclaimed just before everything went black.

CHAPTER 1

LONDON CALLS

"Is this Natasha McMorales?" asked a woman, when Nattie answered the phone. Nattie did not recognize the voice, but knew that it belonged to an older woman. She also knew, or maybe just sensed, that the woman was trying to be amusing.

"This is the Natasha McMorales Detective Agency. I'm Nattie Moreland. Can I help you?" Nattie's answer had become standard practice whenever an inquiry came asking for Natasha McMorales.

"But are you the International PI with the European Sensitivity?"

The woman was clearly trying to establish some level of familiarity with the use of an inside joke. The reference to European sensitivity was a reference Nattie had not heard for over a year. It was a meaningless phrase, but her brother, Kevin, had used it to convince a third generation Italian pastry chef that she was the detective for him. It landed her a missing persons case that turned out to be her agency's big break. It was confusing to hear that phrase now after so much time had passed, especially since so few people knew about it.

"Do I know you?" Nattie asked tentatively, almost embarrassed that she still had not recognized the woman's voice.

"Well, Nattie. I'd like to think we got to know each other fairly well; but in truth, we've only really spent one day together. You were so nice to help an old lady with a bad ankle get around."

"In Florence," Nattie blurted out when she finally realized who the caller was.

"Ah. You remember."

"London!"

"Yes dear. I'm so delighted that you still remember me."

"Still remember you! Of course I remember you. Can you guess what is hanging on the wall behind my desk?"

"A copy of that illegal photograph you took of Michelangelo's *David* at the Academia Museum in Florence?"

London's guess brought a smile to Nattie. Photographs were not allowed in Academia, so she had turned the flash off on her digital camera and had palmed the camera in her right hand while London held on to her left arm. Of the twenty pictures she took of the statue–all taken from the side of her right hip–only three came out well.

"I didn't think you knew about that," confessed Nattie. "I was trying to be inconspicuous."

"Oh, you were very good at it, dear. I would never have known you were taking pictures if I hadn't done the same thing myself."

"That's a pretty good guess." Nattie smiled. She had developed a great affection for London in the day they had spent together. Here was a woman with no airs, no pretenses, and no artificial symbols of status, so unlike her own mother. *If you could pick your own mother, it would be hard to do better than London.*

Nattie continued. "But it's that picture of the Saint Francis statue you sent me from Positano. I told you that I was going to make a poster out of it and I did. I look at it every time I turn on the lights in my office." She laughed. "To tell you the truth, I never developed any of those pictures I took of David."

"Well, you just let me know if you want any of my pictures. I have several."

"Thank you, I will." Then remembering what London had said was her favorite part of the David statue, Nattie asked, "Do you have any shots of his butt?"

"Oh my yes, dear; I certainly do."

Nattie could almost hear London's eyes twinkle. "It sure is nice to hear from you London. How have you been?"

"Well, I've been doing quite nicely for an old lady."

Nattie ignored the 'old lady' remark. "Have you been back to Italy?"

"No, I'm afraid not; but my husband says he wants to go to Rome as soon as he retires."

"Is he going to retire soon?"

"Oh my goodness, I hope not. If he retires, he won't know what to do with himself; and then he'll expect me to entertain him. It would be the end of one of us, and I'm not sure which one."

Nattie laughed.

"How about you dear? Have you been back to Italy?"

"I haven't, but I'd still like to get to Assisi someday and see where Saint Francis came from."

"I'm sure you will get there when the time is right. You are a very resourceful person. If you have a mind to do it, you will."

"Thank you."

"It's just the truth." London paused. "Now tell me about your husband."

Nattie's marital/divorce status was confusing. She still loved him, but she did not trust loving him. He was an alcoholic, but he would not admit it. And he no longer drank, but he owned a bar. She had taken him home after he got knocked out trying to protect her. Intending to nurse him back to good health and send him on his way, she realized that she could not trust her own feelings if she let him get too close. None of this was appropriate to say at the moment but it passed through her mind none-the-less.

"I think you mean Nathan, my ex-husband," corrected Nattie. "He's still my ex-husband, but we get along as well as any divorced folks do."

"I'm glad to hear that, too. If you ask me, I'd say if he doesn't do everything he can to make things right with you, then he's a first class dip-wad."

"I'm not exactly sure what a dip-wad is, London, but could you tell me, are there any men out there that aren't dip-wads?"

"If there are, it's because one of us trained it out of them."

Nattie chuckled. "It is so good to hear from an old friend; I'm glad you called."

London's tone, which had been playful so far, now turned serious. "You don't know how much I wish it was just a call to an old friend, but it isn't. We need a PI."

"Your husband and you?" asked Nattie.

"It's really more my family; I mean *our* family." London now sounded fragile. "Can I ask if you have followed that case of those two authors who were suing each other?"

Nattie had heard about it. The case had received national media attention because it was so unusual. The two men were in a writers' group together. Each had recently published a novel and each was suing the other for libel.

"I think I saw them on the *Today Show* last week sometime. If it's the case I'm thinking of, they were close friends; and they both put each other into their novels. Now they're suing each other for libel."

When Nattie watched the interviews, first with one of the authors and then the other, she was struck by how silly the whole affair was. She wondered about its legitimacy as a news story and remembered thinking, *This is nothing more than two quasi-intellectuals having a squabble.*

"That's that case," London said quietly. "Did you know they were both professors at East Tennessee State University?"

"In Johnson City?"

"Yes."

"No, I didn't. If the *Today Show* did mentioned that I did not catch it. What has all this got to do with you, London?"

London ignored Nattie's question. "Have you heard anything about this case? Today, I mean?"

"No." Nattie's stomach began to knot with anticipation.

"Well, last night Norris Trainor was murdered. And this morning Gil Peters was arrested and charged with the murder."

"And those are the two authors?"

"Yes."

After a long pause, Nattie asked, "London, didn't you once tell me you have a daughter who lives in Johnson City?"

"Yes, I did."

"And her name is Nattie, too, if I remember correctly."

"That's right."

The knot in Nattie's stomach drew tighter still. "Was your son-in-law murdered last night?"

"No," answered London solemnly. "He was arrested this morning."

CHAPTER 2

BREAKFAST WITH KEVIN

Kevin had discovered a new place for breakfast, the Sunny Side Up Grill. Their usual Monday morning spot was Manna Bagel, but the pancakes and country Benedict at Perkins out at Exit 7 on Route 81 made it a favorite spot too. They both liked Blackbird Bakery also, but agreed that it was more of a mid-morning snack place or, if you were a Hobbit, a place second breakfast.

"For a regular old breakfast like Grandma Vee used to make," Kevin noted on the phone, "you can't beat the Sunny Side Up Grill."

Nattie's mouth watered involuntarily, "Eggs, sausage, biscuits, and sawmill gravy?"

"Absolutely. And the coffee is real and the refills are free."

"Boogie Woogie Bugle Boy from Company C" by the Andrews Sisters was playing on the vintage CD player when Nattie walked in. Kevin was sitting at an elevated table next to the window facing Boyd's Bicycle Shop. Across from Kevin, sitting with her back to Nattie, sat a brunette who seemed to be enjoying Kevin's clever repartee.

Kevin called out, "Hey Sis," as Nattie climbed the two steps to their table. "Do you remember Debbie from Science Hill?"

Nattie grit her teeth and stalled to give her memory time to work. Debbie, dressed in a light blue blouse and a dark blue sweater, looked a little like Janine Garofalo, but Nattie still could not place her. "I am usually very good a remembering faces and names. You do look familiar, but I'm sorry, I don't remember your name." Extending her hand, "I'm Nattie Moreland. I was Nattie Johnson in high school."

"And I was Debbie D'Angelo in high school–but that was in Lincoln, Nebraska."

"Ohhhh!" exclaimed Kevin banging his palm on the table. "Why did you tell her so fast? She hadn't squirmed at all yet."

Nattie rolled her eyes at Kevin, but kept her focus on Debbie.

Debbie shrugged. "I'm actually Debbie Duncan now."

"Has anyone ever told you that you look like …"?

"Janine Garofalo," interjected Debbie with a smile. "Actually they usually say I look like I could be her sister."

Grinning, "That's great isn't it? I get, 'You look like you could be Kristen Bell's sister. Not Kristen Bell herself, but her sister."

Debbie leaned back, "You do look like Kristen Bell."

Sitting, "So Debbie Duncan from Nebraska, what brings you to Bristol and how do you know my idiot brother?"

"My husband, Duane, just got out of dental school and got his first job here. Kevin and I were in the fifth grade together."

"And we reconnected through Facebook," offered Kevin.

"I looked for classmates in Bristol, and Kevin's name popped up," explained Debbie.

"Let me guess. You and the Muhammad Ali of practical jokes here have been plotting to set me up to see if I would pretend to remember you from high school?"

Debbie answered with a guilty smile. "She got us," Debbie said to Kevin.

"I told you she was a great detective," beamed Kevin sarcastically.

"It is good to meet you, Nattie. One never knows when one will need a great detective."

"And it is good to meet you too," returned Nattie, shaking her hand. "But you really need to work on upgrading your social network."

"Are you ready to order?" The waitress had appeared at the side of the table unnoticed.

"Pancakes," answered Kevin quickly.

"I think Nattie may need a moment to look at a menu," suggested Debbie.

"I'm fine," said Nattie. "You go ahead."

Debbie handed her menu to the waitress. "Just oatmeal please."

"Can you make scrambled eggs with shredded Swiss cheese?" asked Nattie.

The waitress nodded yes.

"I will have that with hot sauce, wheat toast, bacon, and coffee."

"I'll get your coffee," said the waitress. "Your orders will be up in a minute." Pointing at the edge of the table where a small tin pail holding napkins and condiments, "The hot sauce and syrup are on the table."

After the waitress brought coffee to Nattie and refilled the other two cups, Nattie turned to Debbie. "So you and Kevin were in the fifth grade together."

"Third and forth too."

"I don't suppose you have any embarrassing stories about my brother from those days, do you?"

"Something to even the score?" Debbie asked gleefully rubbing her hands together.

"Wait a minute," demanded Kevin as he put both palm on the table and leaned forward. He looked back and forth between them, "What just happened here?" Neither woman answered, but smiled at him as if he were on display. "I can't believe this." Pushing himself back from the table, "You're here together for three minutes and you're picking on the guy." Leaning forward again and scowling, "It's some kind of a girl thing isn't it?" Patting his shirt pocket as if looking for a pen, "I'm going to have to write that down."

"Mercy," said Debbie in a motherly voice.

Nattie looked at Debbie and nodded her head towards Kevin. "He doesn't really need us for this conversation, so go ahead with your story."

Debbie and Nattie leaned closer together. "I just remember one day when he got sent to the principal's office. It made us laugh."

"Oh good," Nattie smiled broadly, "tell me that story."

"Our fifth grade teacher was an old woman named Mrs. Escopey. She was almost ready to retire I think. She was always telling us how important being a teacher was and what a noble profession it is, which it is."

"Which it is," agreed Nattie.

"But to her teachers did not get enough respect. There was this one day when she was on a tirade about the phrase 'those who can do, those who can't teach.' That phrase would set her off every time she heard it, and we heard about it every time. Apparently someone on the Jay Leno show the night before had said it on television. She came in the next day and told us, 'The phrase should be; those who do, do.'" Pointing across the table with her thumb, "and Kevin here told her, **'Everyone** can do-do.'"

CHAPTER 3

NATTIE REMEMBERS

The drive to the west side of Johnson City where Natalie and Gil Peters lived was a mixture of pleasant memories and sorrow. Long before the developers built the Atlanta Bread Company and all of the other attractions, it had been a farm. It was Frank and Vivian O'Conner's farm. And on that farm is where Nattie's mother Ingrid grew up.

Even when she was a little girl Ingrid O'Conner was embarrassed by her working class parents. She never said as much to her children but it was obvious to Nattie. Ingrid knew what she wanted; she wanted out. Out of her family, off of the farm, into something, anything that would take her away from where she was. That is why she married Nattie's father, Nathan when she was nineteen. It was in the middle of her sophomore year at East Tennessee State University. She had majored in literature because she loved to read, but she had not fared well with her grades because she had been born with a curse. She was beautiful, not glamour model beautiful or Baywatch beautiful, but a cute figure and a farm girl face that men seemed drawn to. Maybe it was her big brown eyes, or the Farrah Fawcett hair that she still made work, or the playful smile with the perfect teeth. Whatever it was, men were attracted to it, and for a woman whose goal was to get out the temptation to use her effect on men was too much to resist. She had charmed her way into collage when the female admission counselor told her high school grades were not good enough. The male director of admissions said, "Everyone needs a second chance." When college became more work than she cared for she wanted out again. That is when Nathan Johnson came along. The irony of both Nattie and her mother marrying alcoholics with the same name was not lost on her.

Neither Frank nor Vivian O'Conner approved of Nathan Johnson. At twenty-six he was not too old for their nineteen year old, but she was still in school and he was in another stage of life. But denying their daughter anything she said she wanted was not in their vocabulary. She was their princess. It was no wonder that she expected to be treated like a princess. The marvel was that she got it to happen. And for Nathan Johnson, a princess was what he wanted. Their marriage was a fairy tale for a long time. They were like children with money. No toy was too expensive and no adventure worth having was worth waiting for as long as the money held out. He had two skills; he could make her laugh and he could make money. Selling x-ray equipment gave him the high commissions that made their life work.

Nattie was their first child. They were not particularly bad parents; they were just unprepared for the full responsibility of caring for another human being. Luckily for them, and Nattie, Nattie was not a difficult child to care for. There were no serious illnesses or obstacles to her growth and development so their parental deficits were more subtle. As long as Nattie was content to be entertained or enjoyed the same things as her parent's, her life was idealic. It was at those moments when Nattie's curiosity took a turn unfamiliar to her mother that the disconnect would occur. So Nattie came to believe what any child would believe in that situation, that her interests were not important, that her uniqueness was not appreciated, and to be connected in her family she had better pay more attention to what her mother wanted than what she needed. And that is when the caretaker role began to take shape in her young life.

The caretaker role got fixed even more when Kevin was born. Nattie was four and was too young to take over the mother role for her brother, but that did not keep her from being over-attentive to what was going on with him. She watched and waited for those golden moments when he needed something she could get. It was her way to demonstrate to her mother that she, Nattie, was needed herself. It was her way to ensure being noticed by her parents. An occasional 'thank you, Nattie' was all she needed to feel her position in the family constellation was secure. The "strategy" worked so well that by the time she was six she could get him up and going in the morning. By the time she was seven he called her mom and Ingrid mommy. To protect her mother's feelings Nattie taught him to call her Sissy.

Until Nattie was eleven her father was a functioning alcoholic. Mostly he was happy just irresponsible when it came to his family. At least that is how she remembered it. He traveled quite a bit, but when he was home he was almost always fun; wrestling with Kevin, clowning with Nattie, and whatever it was he did with Ingrid made her laugh like a little girl. But every so often he would come home different; irritable, withdrawn, and sullen. Nattie would ask what was wrong, but Ingrid just made excuses for him. 'He's tired' and 'he's just stressed' were her common explanations. Once Kevin observed, 'Daddy stinks,' but Ingrid just said, "Natalie, take care of your brother."

Everything changed the day Nathan killed a little girl with his car. He was in Philadelphia. He was supposed to be picking someone up in front their hotel. He did not know the man he was picking up but he had a description so he was driving slowly and looking out the drivers' window. No one had an explanation for why that little girl was just standing in the street but the witnesses said she froze. She was eight. Her name was Martha. Nathan never saw her. He did not know that he had hit her until the car went over her.

Nattie shivered as she remembered wondered what it would feel like to live with a memory like that. Ingrid took Nattie with her to the hearing, but Kevin stayed with the O'Conner grandparents who had come from Johnson City to lend their support. Frank has said he would go to the hearing with her but Ingrid had insisted that only she and Nattie go. On the way to the hearing Ingrid explained, "I don't want them to hear what is said about your father." It seemed reasonable to Nattie at the time. She heard it all. She heard about his blood alcohol level, which was just barely legal but close enough to be mentioned. She heard the lawyers ask him about his drinking and then got to hear him lie. Martha's mother was at the hearing too, and Nattie got to hear her sobbing. And then when it was all over she got to hear what Martha's mother called him, what she screamed at him as they left the courthouse.

After the hearing he stopped being a functioning alcoholic. He was just an alcoholic. Six months later he was unemployed, and that is when he left. Ingrid packed up her kids and returned to the O'Conner farm in Johnson City. If he were coming back they would not be there to receive him. Nattie never asked about her father and she made sure Kevin did not either.

Ingrid had enough money from the divorce to return to college and still provide nicely for herself and her two kids for as long as it took to finish her degree as long as they stayed with her parents. On day ten they moved to an upscale two-bedroom apartment on the other side of Johnson City. Ingrid got a job selling purses from one of the kiosks at The Mall on the weekends, which meant that Nattie and Kevin got to stay on the farm.

Some of the best memories from Nattie's childhood were those weekends on the farm. Friday night was game night with popcorn and hot cocoa. Saturdays always started with a big country breakfast followed by what Grandpa Frank called 'walking the farm,' which was a leisurely walk across and around the whole farmstead. 'This is important work,' Grandpa told Kevin, 'you have to take time to slow down and survey where you are and what needs doing otherwise you will miss what should not be missed.' Kevin believed him. Nattie believed him too, but she suspected that he was walking his grandkids as much as his farm.

The O'Conners attended the Methodist church on Sunday mornings. For Nattie and Kevin this was a new experience for Ingrid and Nathan had never gone or mentioned church. Prior to this Nattie's only exposure to the things of religion was her mother's fascination with Saint Francis. Ingrid never took her children to church, or read the Bible to them, or prayed with them, but there was always a little plastic Saint Francis statue on her dashboard. The story of Saint Francis and the wolf was Nattie's favorite children's story.

The Saint Francis statue, books, and her copy of the "Brother Sun, Sister Moon" movie, all treasured objects, were all abandoned when Lionel O'Brien entered their lives. It was a snow day and the schools were closed so Ingrid took them to the food court at The Mall for lunch. She had forgotten to bring her wallet, but that did not keep her from ordering their meals. She was confident that someone would understand her situation and either take care of them or trust her to come back. 'Never forget how much everyone likes to help damsels in distress,' Ingrid once told Nattie in a moment of motherly instruction. Later when Nattie read Tennessee Williams' *Streetcar Named Desire* she came across the 'I've always depended on the kindness of strangers,' line she put the book down and said, "Oh my goodness, my mother is Blanche DuBois."

The dependable stranger at the food court that snowy day was not the young male manager, which would have been more common, but the older gentleman standing behind them, Lionel O'Brien. 'Put that on this,' he said to the manager as he passed his credit card across the counter. Lionel joined them for lunch. 'I am a lawyer,' he told them.

'I just knew you were a nice man when I saw you enter the food court,' Ingrid openly flirted, 'I even said it out loud.'

'I don't remember that,' observed Kevin

'I do,' lied Nattie, backing up her mother's story.

Within a week Ingrid was working as a receptionist at the Skinner, Watson, and O'Brien law firm. No one will ever know what kind of receptionist skills Ingrid had because three months after beginning that career she was forced to retire. Apparently the other partners were concerned that a receptionist being engaged to one of the founding partners might create some tensions amongst the staff. Three months later Ingrid and Lionel were married. The six-month courtship was one month longer than Nattie had predicted to her Grandma Vee after she discovered that Lionel had been a widower for four years.

Nattie realized that in many ways Lionel O'Brien is a good man; intelligent, generous, and stable. The difficulty with Lionel, if difficulty was the right word, was that he had very definite ideas about many things coupled with a self-assurance that gave him license to voice his opinions, "persuasively." It was not that his persuasion mattered in the least to Ingrid, for she absorbed his world view without question, but it mattered to Nattie a great deal who had already surrendered her childhood needs to her mother and did not intend to surrender her adulthood judgment to her mother's "man." The struggle between Nattie and Lionel over Nattie's right to her own thoughts, values, and preferences, a struggle Lionel was oblivious to, began over Saint Francis. Lionel's church, the

Westfield Independent Church was a very conservative church with a strong anti-Catholic bias that Nattie could not understand. And she really could not understand when her mother took her life long affection for Saint Francis and threw it all away just because Lionel did not agree. To make matters worse, Lionel did not try to persuade Ingrid to get rid of her Saint Francis paraphernalia, she just did it on her own. Nattie would have done anything for anyone in discomfort, if for no other reason than to avoid the guilt of not doing so, but giving up a part of yourself to please a man was, to her, a supreme act of self-degradation.

Moving into the O'Brien home was not all bad. It was a large home in an affluent neighborhood, where Lionel had lived with his first wife, Pat. Pat and Lionel had one child together, a daughter named Samantha. Sam was three years older than Nattie, so Nattie not only got her own bedroom, she got a big sister. Sam could not have been more welcoming; she personally decorated Nattie's room before Nattie moved in, which was very nice because she had great taste. Sam also picked out a closet full of clothes and introduced Nattie to her friends. Sam would have been a dream big sister if only she had been a person herself. As far as Nattie could tell, Samantha was a walking talking fourteen year old female version of Lionel. With Ingrid rapidly become a thirty-three year old female version of Lionel herself Nattie was determined to resist the hypnotic temptation. And if it were within her power, she would keep Kevin from drinking the Kool-aid too.

One of the key hypnotic techniques was the ritual of a formal lunch every Sunday after church. A ritual that continues still even though all the kids, including Samantha, had grown and moved out of the house. They kept their Sunday clothes on and ate in the dining room instead of the kitchen. The unspoken rule was that after eating lunch Lionel would ask each of them a question about their life and they each got a turn to talk about whatever he had asked about. Once each of them, including Ingrid, had had a turn to speak he would lean back in his chair and say that something one of us said reminded him of something he had been thinking about. His pontifications could last anywhere from fifteen to forty-five minutes, even longer if someone asked a question. He was a very intelligent man whose opinions were all well thought out and well articulated. He was sure he was always right and he generally was. He was also sure that he was interesting, but that was one thing he did not get right.

It appeared to be Lionel's status rather than his wealth that so attracted Ingrid. Wealth was still important to Ingrid, but status was more so. This was seen most vividly by the fact that she continued to be embarrassed by her parents even after they became wealthy selling off parcels of their farm. It was several sales that in the end gave them a net worth of $1,500,000. Each time they sold a section of property it was developed, which only increased the value of the next section they sold. Grandpa Frank was not a shrewd negotiator; he took what they offered and never questioned if he could have held out for more. What he got was so much more than he needed or expected that he always agreed.

Wealth had not agreed with Frank or Vivian. They missed working, so they began another business building wooden fences for homeowners. They didn't make much money at the fence business, but enough for Ingrid's brother, Keith, to make a living. Eventually, it was a part-time concern for Frank and Vivian, and they volunteered the rest of their time to the likes of Habitat for Humanity and the Haven of Rest in Bristol.

Ingrid got her wish for more money when, after Nattie's senior year of high school, Frank, Vivian, and Keith were all killed in a traffic accident. It is not that Ingrid wished for their death. Nattie knew that. But it bothered her that it did not take her mother long to begin thinking of how that money would affect her. Nattie knew this about her mother because, much to her chagrin, she had the same thoughts herself.

But her grandparents' money did not free them from the dependence upon her stepfather, as Nattie had hoped. The inheritance meant more money, but it was not more status. As far as Nattie and Kevin were concerned, the money had the strange affect of increasing Ingrid's dependence on Lionel. His interest in Nattie and her brother had been mostly to convert them to his religious beliefs, but other than that he had left them alone.

With a sizable fortune at stake, Lionel suddenly had more opinions about how they were raised. "Unearned money makes people lazy" was a common theme of his lectures. Thus, when he set up trust funds for Nattie and Kevin, he placed himself as executor of each trust. This meant that other than a monthly allowance of $500, Kevin received no benefit from his share of the inheritance. The stated reason? "If he has the money, he'll never go to college." The truth was that with or without the money Kevin was not going to college. Although probably a creative genius, Kevin did not have an attention span conducive to formal education. He might have benefited from treatment for Attention Deficit Disorder, but Lionel did not believe in psychological "excuses." And if Lionel did not believe an education in psychology was a worthy enterprise then Ingrid did not either

It struck Nattie as odd that Lionel blamed the money for Kevin's decision to skip college when it was more likely his own attitude towards psychology that was responsible. That same attitude was responsible for Nattie's leaving college after her sophomore year. She had declared psychology as her major, but without money from the trust fund could not afford to continue after she lost a scholarship when she took the blame for her roommate's violation of college regulations about alcohol in the dormitory. Although this ended her life as a student, it was the beginning of her transition into her career as a PI–a choice Lionel also disapproved of, but a choice he could not prevent.

It all boiled down to this; whatever a kid was supposed to get from their parents, Nattie was short-changed. But the attention, acceptance, and affirmation she got from Frank and Vee O'Conner went a long way towards making up the deficit. With a touch of defiance Nattie thought, *My grandparents would have been proud of me*, as she turned into the Peters neighborhood.

CHAPTER 4

NATTIE MEETS WITH GIL PETERS

Natalie and Gil lived in an attractive two-story condominium that looked pretty new to Nattie compared to the thirty year old bungalow she rented. Before Nattie turned her car off in the driveway, she noticed the front door to the house being opened by a woman she assumed was London's daughter. The woman stepped out on the landing and folded her arms across her stomach. Natalie was a younger version of her mother. True, the daughter's hair was longer and her body more athletic than the slender figure of her mother. The face, however, was the same, with the striking clear blue eyes.

"Natasha?" she called out as Nattie got out of her car. "Natasha Morales?"

"Actually, it's McMorales," Nattie corrected the incorrect pronunciation of the incorrect name without realizing that it would complicate her eventual explanation of her name. "But please call me Nattie."

When Nattie got close enough she could see Natalie's swollen eyes, pale skin, and the beginnings of a cold sore on the corner of her mouth. Offering her hand, "And you are Nattie, aren't you?"

"My mother calls me Nattie, but I prefer Natalie. You can call me Nattie if you want. Come on in."

The two shook hands, and Nattie stepped through the doorway and into their living room, which was decorated in an Americana style with a simple couch and chair and several large wooden cabinets and tables.

"You have a lovely home, Natalie."

"Thank you. Please sit down and make yourself comfortable. I'll get my husband."

Gil and Natalie sat together on the couch and held each other's hands. Gil was dressed in khaki pants and a button down striped shirt. His hair was wet. Overall he looked less un-nerved than his wife. Nattie noticed another difference between them, while Natalie sat and stared directly at her, somewhat like a deer mesmerized by the headlights of an oncoming car, Gil could not seem to maintain eye contact for more than a moment or two, before looking at his wife or around the room.

Nattie, sitting across from them, started by saying, "London and I talked briefly last night. I know that you have been arrested–" The comment made both of them flinch. "–And that you have been accused of killing a Norris Trainor. Is that correct?"

"He did not do it," Natalie protested.

Gil patted her hand. "But I was arrested for it." He turned to Nattie. "This is all very strange to us, Ms McMorales, and we are more than a little on edge; but we appreciate any help you can give us. Ask us anything you need to know."

"She needs to know that you didn't do it, Gil."

Both Nattie and Gil smiled at Natalie's assertion.

"She's right, of course. The most important thing for you to know is that I did not kill Norris. We were friends." Then to his wife, he added, "We can't expect her to just believe us. We need to let her do her job her way."

Natalie frowned.

"Thank you, Mr. Peters."

"My friends call me Gil."

"And mine call me Nattie. Now suppose you tell me what you know."

Gil cleared his throat, and, letting go of his wife's hand, shifted in his seat. "I'm not sure where to begin, so I'll start at what happened last night if that is okay?"

Nattie took a notebook and pen out of her bag.

"Norris was killed two nights ago. Someone hit him in the head in the parking lot of a tavern out towards Barley Corners. There were eighty dollars and two credit cards in his wallet, and his car keys were still in his pocket." He paused and looked at Nattie for guidance.

"It wasn't a robbery. Go on."

"Well, that's really it. I did not know anything about it until yesterday morning when two cops showed up at our door."

"They were very rude," Natalie insisted.

Gil gave Nattie an apologetic look. "In a way I am the natural suspect."

"Why do you say that, Gil?"

"Norris and I were suing each other, so it is natural for the police to assume there was animosity between us."

"Was there animosity between you?"

"No. None at all."

"But you were taking each other to court?"

Gil looked at his wife, who nodded her approval.

"The suits were phony. They were publicity stunts to promote our novels. I hesitate for that to get out because I do not know how much trouble we would be in if that became public knowledge." He blinked and turned to take Natalie's hand again. "I mean I do not know how much trouble Norris and I would be in."

Nattie waited for Gil to turn back towards her. "I know this is difficult for you, but surely you are aware that you are in considerable trouble now."

"I know," he said, shaking his head in embarrassment.

"Tell me more about the lawsuits."

"Norris and I and three other professors from East Tennessee State University used to meet a couple of evenings a month. We are all writers. We would take turns presenting what we were working on to each other."

"But it was just you and Norris Trainor who were in the lawsuits?"

"Yes. Only Norris and I were working on novels. Brandon is a song writer, Tommy writes plays, and Andy integrates science fiction classics with higher mathematics."

"How do you integrate science fiction and math?"

Gil shrugged. "To tell you the truth, none of the rest of us understood the math parts."

"But it was only you two novelists who were suing each other."

"That's right. A character in my novel was based on Norris; and he had one in his novel that was based on me. We were suing one another for defamation of character."

"But the suits were phony?"

"Absolutely," piped in Natalie.

"Can you prove that they were phony?"

"Norris was an economist. In his novel he imagined a utopian society that was based on the Nation of Israel as it was meant to be."

"I don't understand."

"He supposed that if this nation kept the Year of Jubilee, as Israel was supposed to do, then our economic system, which is largely based upon interest, could not have developed the way it has."

"Year of Jubilee?"

"The Year of Jubilee was a year in which all debts were forgiven. If the Jewish people had incorporated it into their economy it would have changed how they lent and borrowed money. Norris' book was set on the present, but with a completely different economic system."

Nattie nodded her head with an enthusiasm she did not feel. *If I read that on the back cover of a book I would never buy it.*

"I know what you are thinking."

She raised an eyebrow.

"It sounds boring, but that is because I did not explain it well. It is a really good read. Norris was a great writer. His characters were interesting, and he had several overlapping plot lines."

"And there was a character based on you?"

"Yes, an English literature professor who specialized in Southern literature."

"And that is what you are? An English lit prof specializing in– What?"

"Southern literature. You know. Faulkner."

"So that is clearly you. What did he name you?"

Both Natalie and Gil looked at her like the answer should be obvious.

"Gil? He based a character on you and gave him your name?"

Gil nodded. "I did the same thing in my novel. My main character is an unconventional econ professor who clashes with the head of his department because the students like him."

"And you named him Norris, right?"

"Right."

"So there was a basis for libel suits. Could you not have avoided all of this by just using different names and different educations?"

"We could have, but we didn't want to avoid the lawsuits. We wanted to set them up."

"Are you telling me that suing each other was the plan from the beginning?" She lowered her voice, "You will have to explain that to me."

"Suing each other was not from the very beginning, but we knew it would be hard to get a publisher to look at our books. Neither of us had published anything other than our dissertations. We needed something extra to get us noticed."

"Counter libel suits would surely get you noticed."

Gil nodded sheepishly.

"And of course that libel suit is the motive the police are basing their case on?"

Gil nodded.

"Well, that should be easy to get around. I assume the other three men in your writers group will back up your story."

Gil's head dropped.

Raising her eye brow, "They did not know, did they?"

"No. No one knew except Gil and me. I told Natalie, but I did not tell anyone else. I do not know if he told his wife, but we agreed that letting anyone else in on it was too risky. You know, the *Today Show* interviewed us because of it. It was a pretty short interview on separate satellite feeds but they would never have even done that if there was a hint of its being a stunt."

"It was Norris' idea," asserted Natalie.

Gil looked at her disapprovingly.

Leaning back with a pleading look on her face, "Well it was."

Gil turned back towards Nattie. "I don't suppose it matters, but it was Gil's idea in the first place."

"At this point, I have no idea what does and does not matter. "

"Can you help us?" Natalie held tight to her husband's arm. "We are desperate. Gil can't go back to work. We are afraid to leave the house."

Nattie could not picture Gil killing anyone, much less his friend. She noticed that he had been more excited talking about his friend's novel than he was about his own. *Would a murderer do that?* she wondered.

"It would have been better if we could get corroboration that you were not really mad at each other. Without that, I will just have to figure out who did it. Someone killed him, and whoever it was probably had a reason, it will be a lot easier to find out who the killer is if I can figure out why him."

CHAPTER 5

NATTIE GOES TO THE POLICE

The logical place to begin looking for a motive for murder was always with the spouse of the deceased, so naturally Nattie asked, "What can you tell me about Norris Trainor's wife.

"Her name is Callie," answered Gil. "I suppose most people would describe her as attractive but cold and distant."

"She never showed the slightest interest in getting to know any of the other faculty or their families," stated Natalie. "At least she never showed any interest in getting to know me."

Gil confirmed his wife's observation. "Me either. You could make pleasant conversation with her, but she never revealed anything intimate about herself."

"And if others revealed something intimate about themselves, she would never follow up with a question or do anything to show that she had been listening."

"Do you think she could have done it?" asked Nattie tentatively.

Gil and Natalie looked at each other as if this possibility had not crossed either of their minds. "Naaaa," they both agreed at the same time.

Trying to get information from the family of the recently deceased was one of the most unpleasant aspects of investigation work, and Nattie hated to do it. She had been lucky so far inasmuch as the Natasha McMorales Private Investigation Agency had not been called upon to perform this particular duty. But when she worked for Hiram Moreland, that duty always fell to her. "This is one of your gifts," Hiram had insisted.

Is it not an amazing coincidence that the "gifts" men notice most in women tends to correspond to the tasks they do not want to do?

After getting Callie Trainor's phone number and address, Nattie excused herself and went to her car to make the phone call.

The phone stopped ringing after just three rings, but there was a long pause before a woman said, "Yes," in a barely audible voice.

"Is this Mrs. Callie Trainor?"

"Who is this?"

"My name is Nattie Moreland. I'm a PI from Bristol. I am investigating the horrible tragedy that has fallen on the Trainor family. If you are Mrs. Trainor, then I would very much like to talk to you. Are you Mrs. Trainor?"

Pause. "I am."

"Well Mrs. Trainor, let me say that I am dreadfully sorry for your loss and I know talking to me is the last thing you want to do, but if you could spare me just a little time it will go a long way in helping my investigation."

Pause. "Are you with the police?"

"No, ma'am. I am a PI."

Pause "I don't know."

Nattie held silent.

"What time is it now?"

Looking at her watch, "It's 11:00."

Pause. "Come by at 3:00."

"Could we make it …." Nattie stopped talking as she realized Callie Trainor was no longer on the phone.

With four hours to kill, Nattie decided to have lunch at Café One 11 where the lunch prices fit her financial sensitivities better than the dinner prices did. She could taste the sushi roll and the edamame just by picturing them. But first she would go by the Johnson City Police Station and pick up a copy of the arrest report and the charges.

"Alan Poe," was the answer Nattie received when she asked who the arresting officer was in the Norris Trainor case. It was not the answer Nattie wanted to hear. She had been a sophomore at Science Hill High School when Alan Poe was a senior. As a senior, Alan was the second-string quarterback. It was said that he was wiry, which Nattie took to mean that he was stronger than he looked. Nattie also took it that his position on the football team made him a member of the A group. She thought of herself as somewhere in the D group range, which made her suspicious of anyone in the A group. When Alan, who had never spoken to her before, invited her to go to a graduation party, her response was not only harsh, but, as she found out later, also cruel. "I don't have time for a family of morphine freaks." What she thought was a clever reference to Edgar Alan Poe, whom Alan Poe was not even remotely related to, hit Alan much closer to home than she knew.

"Sorry to bother you," was all he said as he walked away from her. It was the last time she ever saw him. It was not until Nattie's junior year that she discovered that Alan had lost his father to suicide after years of struggling with a heroin addiction. And now fate was bringing them together again.

"Are you Ms Moreland?" asked a uniformed officer from the doorway. It was Alan. At least this policeman had Alan's face, but this man was more filled out than Alan ever was. This was a very fit, very athletic thirty-two-year-old man.

"I'm Nattie Moreland."

He showed no sign of recognizing her. "Follow me please, ma'am."

Oh good, she thought. *He called me ma'am.*

He led her to a small room and ushered her to a chair on one side of a small table. He waited for Nattie to sit before he took the seat across from her. Taking the file folder from under his arm he placed it on the table and folded his hands over the top of it. "What is this about?"

"As I told the desk sergeant, I am a PI from Bristol and I am looking into the death of Norris Trainor."

"Who is your client?"

"I have been hired by the family of the accused."

His eyebrows rose for a moment. Nattie read that to mean he did not think much about her chances. "I see," was all he said before adjusting the folder in front of him. "Would you like to see what we have?"

"Yes please, that would be helpful."

"Actually, I do not think that it will be much help to you but you are entitled to know what the evidence is."

Nattie leaned against the table, "Before we do that, Officer Poe, could I ask you a personal question?"

When his expression did not change in the slightest, she wondered if he had recognized her. She was using a different last name and the dozen years since high school had changed her a bit as well. But she asked anyway, "Do you remember me from high school?"

"Should I?"

"Science Hill? You were in the Class of '96?"

"Yes. Did we graduate together?"

"No. I was in the class of '98, and we did not really know each other, but you asked me out once. It was near graduation. Are you sure you don't remember me?"

Officer Poe squinted and leaned forward, taking a closer look before shaking his head, "No, I am sorry, I don't remember. I hope I was a gentleman."

"Oh you were a perfect gentleman." Nattie sat back. "I was the wretch, I'm afraid."

"Really?"

Nattie nodded. "Really. I was a little suspicious of why you were asking me out; so when you did, my reaction was way out of line. I have regretted it for a long time."

Alan showed no signs of recognition.

"I was two years behind you, and I hardly traveled in the same social circles as the A group."

He smiled, "I think you have me confused with someone else. I was never in the A crowd."

She eyed him with disbelief. "Football? Quarterback?"

"I was second string, but I never hung out with that group."

It was Nattie's turn to knit her eyebrows. "No, I think it was you."

"I really do not remember, Ms Moreland. Why is it so important?"

"I said something to you that was in really bad taste, and I wanted to apologize."

He hesitated. "That is very thoughtful; but like I said, it wasn't me. Now, did you want to discuss this case?"

"Sure," she said with a mixture of feelings. It was definitely him. *How many Alan Poes could there be?* She was glad that he was not carrying an emotional scar from the incident, but she also felt a little disappointed that he did not remember her at all.

"Okay then." Alan opened the file. "Norris Trainor was found in the parking lot of Never Tell Tavern. The cause of death was a single blow to the head with a round object, most likely a small pipe or something round like that but smaller than a baseball bat. The coroner places the time of death between 9:00 and midnight. That location is outside the Barley Corners city limits, but the Sheriff's Office was tied up with a large traffic accident on 26 so the Barley Corners PD responded to the call." Looking up at Nattie, he added, "Since the deceased and the murderer are both from Johnson City, they were more than happy to shift the case over to us."

"Are you the detective?"

"No, I am not the detective on this case." His voice was sheepish.

"Are you filling in for the detective?"

"I am not a detective yet. I passed the exam six months ago, and I am in line for the next desk, but I'm not a detective yet."

"Okay, Officer Poe. Then who is?"

"That has not been assigned yet."

"Are you telling me that no detective has been assigned to this case, but Gil Peters has been charged anyway? Do you guys usually base an arrest on sketchy circumstantial evidence and no formal investigation?"

"The initial investigation was done by Barley Corners and the evidence is circumstantial, but I would hardly call it sketchy."

"Counter lawsuits that are several months old are exactly what I would call sketchy."

"I don't know anything about counter lawsuits," said Alan, "but Barley Corners places Mr. Peters and Mr. Trainor in that tavern together until 10:15. Mr. Peters left first. Mr. Trainor left at 10:30. He was found an hour and a half later. No one entered or left the establishment between 10:30 and midnight."

Nattie had to force herself to breathe. She looked around the room for something to focus on besides Alan Poe but the walls were starkly bare. *Keep breathing,* she told herself as she digested the evidence against her client and wondered why he had withheld it from her.

"Are you okay?" he asked.

Nattie regained her composure. "I am. Thank you. This was very helpful. Is there anything else I should know?"

"I think that is everything. If you want copies of the arrest report and the charges, you will have to get them from your client's lawyer."

"I understand." Nattie knew the drill. She stood and held out her hand. "Thanks again."

"No problem."

He led her back out the way they had come in. As she stepped through the door he was holding open, he spoke. "Oh Nattie." His voice was softer.

"Yes?" She turned back to face him.

"I do remember you."

Nattie just stared at him.

With just the trace of a smile, he said, "Thank you."

CHAPTER 6

A VERY LONG THREE HOURS

A leisurely healthy lunch had to be savored, and that required a settled mind. The kind of food a restless mind wanted was whatever could be eaten quickly and with as little an audience as possible. That meant Nattie would not be lunching at Café One 11. Instead, she sought out the first fast-food parking lot that did not have a line of cars backed up at the drive-through window.

She had three hours to kill before her next commitment at Callie Trainor's home; but after what she had learned at the police station, she was not so sure she was going to keep that appointment. She needed time to digest the new information; for now, though, she was going to digest some carbohydrates. First the carbs, then the decision. She ordered a Big Burger, fries, and a chocolate shake at the Pals drive-thru, then drove to the boat ramp near Winged Deer Park, where she parked her car in the shade.

Nattie made a point of avoiding thought while she finished off her burger, which she ate with only a few fries. The shake she left alone until after she had deposited the majority of the fries and the other debris in a nearby dumpster. She carried the shake towards the river and sat down on the grass. It was time to think through what she was going to do next.

She had been hired to establish an accused man's innocence. It was a job that she had no interest in unless the accused man was in fact innocent. Normally, she would be neutral; but she really wanted this particular accused man to be innocent because he happened to be the son-in-law of someone she cared about. She wanted Gil Peters to be innocent for London's sake. And although she had believed that he was innocent when she met him earlier that day, she could have been influenced by her desire to protect London. Gil's explanation of the evidence against him had been believable, but incomplete. Now, she not only had new, more damaging information, but she was also suspicious of what she had been told. Was omitting the information about being with the deceased just before he was murdered a lie, an omission, or something else? It felt like a lie.

Being with the deceased just before he was killed meant that Gil had opportunity. On the other hand, it did not mean he had motive, nor did it mean he did it. The case against Gil Peters was still just circumstantial, and there was a gross absence of standard investigation procedure. But withholding the information about being together was just suspicious. Actually was not merely suspicious, it was stupid, *Surely he had to know I would find this out.*

In the end, none of this mattered. London was her friend and this was her son-in-law. That did not mean that she was going to protect a guilty man. And it did not mean she believed he was innocent because, at this point, she was convinced he was not. What it meant was that she had no intention of telling London that she was dropping the case before she could say she had checked out every other reasonable possibility. That meant keeping her 3-o'clock appointment with Callie Trainor.

After throwing the untouched shake in the dumpster, Nattie drove to Barnes and Noble where she bought *The Girl With the Dragon Tattoo* by Stieg Larsson and *One For The Money* by Janet Evanovich. She bought a large coffee and killed an hour reading *One For The Money*.

CHAPTER 7

NATTIE MEETS GREG TAYLOR AT CALLIE'S HOUSE

The Trainors lived in a modest two-story colonial in an older neighborhood near the East Tennessee State University campus. The house looked dark. Parked on the street in front of the house was an old red Mustang. Nattie pulled into the driveway and turned off her car. Before opening the car she sighed, she was fearful that after waiting nearly three hours for Mrs. Trainor to return from wherever she had been, she would have to wait longer.

As Nattie reached the top step, the front door opened and an attractive man dressed in jeans and a dark blue tee shirt stepped out onto the porch. "Ms Moreland, I presume," he stated rather than asked. "I am Greg Taylor."

"Nattie Moreland, yes. I have an appointment with Mrs. Trainor at 3 o'clock. Is she here?"

Greg Taylor was a good eight inches taller than Nattie, and he stood close enough to her to accentuate his height. Normally, this would have felt like a display of power, but not this time. Greg Taylor had big brown eyes that just seemed to make contact with her. He did not ogle her, nor did he try to intimidate her. He was friendly. Her first guess was that this was Mrs. Trainor's brother come to help his sister in her hour of need.

"Please, come on in, Ms Moreland."

She followed him into the foyer of the house, where he turned and gestured towards a formal living room. Before proceeding, she paused to admire a framed photograph hanging on the foyer wall to her left. The mountain scene looked vaguely familiar to her. A road in the foreground disappeared into a curve while the background was layered with several rows of mountains, each a different hue. She wondered if she had seen it in a movie or on a calendar.

She pointed to the picture. "Where is this?"

Greg's mouth opened slightly, and he leaned forward a bit. Rather than answering her, though, he pulled back and motioned once again towards the living room. "Let's have a seat in here."

As he sat in a chair to her left, she repeated her question. "Is Mrs. Trainor here?"

He smiled warmly. "I should probably explain my presence here. I am the Trainors' lawyer." He looked down, almost embarrassed by his statement. "I must apologize, Ms Moreland. I know you came here in good faith expecting to talk to Mrs. Trainor; but after you talked with her this morning, she called my office and– Well, to make a long story short, she is a very private person and she has just gone through a traumatic experience. I am sure you understand. She is under a doctor's care and prefers to have us, I mean me, handle her affairs."

This obstacle to her interview with Callie Trainor was not entirely unexpected. What widow would want to talk to a Private Investigator working for the accused? But after waiting four hours for the time chosen by the widow and after a greeting from someone she had supposed to be a charming brother, Nattie thought she was in. That is why the roadblock caught her so off guard. All she could think to say was, "You don't look like a lawyer."

He laughed. It was a hearty laugh, but not at her expense. "I think I will take that as a compliment," he said holding his hand against his chest. "I assume you are referring to my attire. I was taking a scuba lesson over at South Holston Lake. I did not get the message from my office until an hour ago, so I came without changing into my lawyer outfit."

35

"I did not mean to be offensive Mr. Taylor–"

"Not at all, Ms Moreland. Not at all. The truth is, I do not look much like a lawyer even when I have the costume on."

Nattie was aware of how clever, engaging, and attractive Greg Taylor was; but after waiting half a day to talk to Callie Trainor, she was in no mood to be charmed. Her face must have shown it.

"I am sorry for the inconvenience, but as her attorney I am authorized to represent her interest. So as to not waste any more of your time, do you mind telling me what your business with Mrs. Trainor is?"

Nattie handed him a business card. "I am a PI. I have been hired to investigate what happened to her husband."

He looked at the card and then at Nattie. "Is it Natalie Moreland or Natasha McMorales?"

"I am Natalie Moreland, but please call me Nattie. Natasha McMorales is simply the name of my detective agency."

He pursed his lips. "I see. It is your agency." He put the card on the coffee table. "I think you have a very catchy name for your agency." Then he leaned forward with his elbows on his knees. "What exactly are you investigating? The police have already arrested someone; and as I understand it, they have a very good case."

"As I explained to Mrs. Trainor when I arranged for this meeting, I was hired by the family of the accused. "

"Well," he said, sitting back, "that is probably why she called our office. I know you are just doing your job, but to her it looks like you are trying to defend the man who killed her husband. I'm sure you can understand her point of view."

Nattie leaned forward and opened her mouth to object.

Before she could speak, however, he held up his hand. "You and I both know that an honest investigation will further convict him if he is guilty or will redirect us if he is innocent."

"I was just going to make that point myself," she said as she relaxed and leaned back against the couch. "Frankly I do not know if the accused is guilty or not. If my investigation proves his guilt, then so be it. But the case against him is circumstantial."

"Circumstantial does not mean that it is not a strong case, Ms. Moreland. That is a common misunderstanding of the law. Most convictions are circumstantial."

"I understand that. But even with circumstantial evidence, other possibilities should be investigated and eliminated."

"Other reasonable possibilities," he repeated, emphasizing the word "reasonable." "And I am sure that the police will do just that if they have not done so already."

"That is just it. Their case against Mr. Peters is based on opportunity alone. That is a weak case and that is why I would like so much to speak with Norris Trainor's widow."

"To see if she could help you establish motive?"

"Exactly!"

He smiled again. "I can tell you are very good at your job, Ms Moreland. In fact, I will keep your card for future reference. But as far as this case is concerned, I think you are heading down a rabbit hole. You see, the hostility between Mr. Trainor and Mr. Peters has been well established. They were suing each other, for heaven's sake. If that is not motive, then I do not know what is."

Nattie was not sure of what to do next, but she was sure that she would not be getting past Greg Taylor to interview Callie Trainor today.

"I wish there was something I could do," he said apologetically, "but I have to respect Mrs. Trainor's wishes. Perhaps you could get more information about the evidence the police have from your client's lawyer."

"That is a good suggestion. Thank you. Mr. Peters has not hired counsel yet, but I plan on suggesting that the next time I speak with him."

Greg Taylor opened the front door and followed Nattie onto the porch. "I have been practicing in Johnson City for only about eighteen months. Still, I have probably run across most of the law firms in town. Do you need any suggestions for your client?"

"That is above and beyond the call of duty, Mr. Taylor, and I appreciate it, but I think I will recommend my step-father's law firm."

"Your step-father is a lawyer here in town?"

"Yes. Skinner, O'Brien, and Watson. Have you heard of them?"

"I have," he said. "That's where I work."

CHAPTER 8

RETURN TO GIL PETERS

It was surprising when, at 4:15, no one answered Nattie's knock on the Peters' front door. Based on what Natalie Peters had said earlier about being afraid to leave the house, it was likely they would be back soon. What she had to say needed to be said in person, but what she was going to say had changed several times. When she drove away from their home the first time, she was going to accept the job; but after she left the Police station she was not. Then she went to the river and decided to take a chance; but after talking to Greg Taylor, she decided she had no chance. It was the car. Every time she got in the car she changed her mind.

She decided to wait for them to return but when she got to her car she paused and asked herself, *If I get in this car now, am I going to change my mind again?*

Just as she touched the door handle, her cell phone rang. It was London Southerland. *That answers that,* she thought and got in her car before she answered her phone.

"Hi, London."

"Before we go any further, Nattie, I want you to know that I am not going to be calling you all the time, bugging you about how it is going."

Nattie could hear the tension in London's voice. "I just needed to tell you to send the bill to my husband's office."

"Hi, London," Nattie repeated.

London exhaled. Her next words were spoken more calmly. "But as long as I have you on the phone let me ask; How is it going?"

"So far I have met with your kids and the arresting officer and the lawyer for widow of the deceased, and now I am waiting for your daughter and her husband to get home."

"How is it going?"

"I don't know. Gil does not look like he could commit murder and I don't buy the motive that has been attributed to him." To herself she added, *But most murderers don't look like they could be murderers and my not buying the lawsuit motive does not mean he does not have another motive we don't know about.*

"That means you will take the case, right?"

It was not the question Nattie wanted to hear. "I am not sure yet. The police believe they have a strong case. It is circumstantial, though, and I still have to determine if they are checking into other possibilities. As for other possibilities, the widow is the logical place to start looking for other motives."

"Do you think it could have been his wife?"

"She has to be eliminated as a suspect, but I am sure the police will at least do that. For my part, even if she is not guilty, she might know whether someone had a motive to kill her husband. She might know something that she does not know is something. But I have reached a dead end with Callie Trainor; she has her lawyer keeping me away."

"They can't do that." Now London sounded exasperated. "Can they?"

"I can not force her to talk to me. I am going to suggest that Gil get a lawyer. Maybe his lawyer can force her to open up, but I cannot."

"Can you– trick her?" asked London sheepishly.

Nattie laughed. "Do you have something in mind?"

"I don't know, but I do know it is not fair for someone with information about this simply to decide not to talk about it without a good reason. Does she have a good reason?"

"I don't know if she has a good reason, but that would be a good thing for me to find out," Nattie mused as she watched Gil and Natalie Peters turn into their driveway. "Listen, London I need to get off the phone. Gil just got home. He and I have a few loose ends to tie up before I make a decision about taking on anymore of this investigation."

Natalie was not shy in expressing her displeasure about being sent inside while Nattie and Gil spoke; but when she finally shut the front door, Nattie turned to Gil. "Tell me about that tavern in Barley Corners."

"You mean where Norris was found?"

Instead of answering, Nattie glared at him. She wanted him to know she was angry. He knew very well which tavern she meant.

"It is called the Never Tell Tavern," answered Gil. "With the lawsuits still going on, Norris and I met at some out-of-the-way place about every week or so. We did not want to risk being seen in town together. Is that what you wanted to know?"

"You met every couple of weeks, is that right?"

"Yes."

Natalie waited expecting him to explain, but eventually asked, "Why?"

Looking down, "No reason really, we were just friends, and we talked about what we were writing."

"And why was it so important to avoid being seen together?"

"That was more Norris' concern than mine. He thought it would hurt our lawsuit."

The bogus lawsuit that was just a publicity stunt?"

"Right." Pleadingly adding, "I swear."

They were both silent while Nattie looked intently into his eyes and he held his breath.

When she relaxed and looked away, he relaxed too. Breathing deeply, "What else do you want to know?"

"What I want to know is anything and everything I need to know to do my job, and I do not want to have to ask for it. Now, is there anything else I should know?"

Gil looked down. "I can't think of anything." After a moment, he looked up again, his eyes pleading. "I didn't know it was important. I was there with Norris, but I left earlier than he did. The bartender saw me leave; he could back me up."

"Did he see you leave the bar or the parking lot?"

Gil frowned.

"Did anyone see you leave the parking lot?"

He shook his head.

"Gil, do you understand that the whole case against you is that the police can place you in that bar just before Norris was murdered?"

He shrugged. "I didn't take it very serious, I'm afraid. I didn't do it. There has to be evidence that someone else did."

She turned her head away from him. He was right about that. If he did not do it, then there had to be evidence that someone else did; and that evidence would not get found if no one was looking for it. Turning back towards him she held up a finger. "First thing tomorrow get yourself a good lawyer and confess–first thing–to your phony lawsuits. If you hold on to that secret too long, you risk credibility. Then I want you to think real hard about what I need to know because if I find out that you knew something but did not tell me, then I am done. I mean it, Gil. I don't care who your mother-in-law is. If you withhold anything else, that will be it for me. Do we understand each other?"

He nodded vigorously. "Understood."

"Good. Now I am going home and taking the rest of the day off."

"And tomorrow?"

"Tomorrow?" London's suggestion flitted before her mind. "I have a few tricks up my sleeve for tomorrow."

CHAPTER 9

NATTIE AND NATE VISIT HIRAM AT HOSPITAL

Taking the rest of the day off was not in the cards, however, because as she was driving back to Bristol, her phone rang.

"Hello, Nathan," she answered. Her ex-husband's ring tone on her phone was the song "I Won't Grow Up" from Peter Pan.

"Hello, Nat. Where are you?"

"I am working, Nate. What do you need?"

"Well, for starters, I'd appreciate you returning my phone calls."

"I have been very busy, Nate. Did you need something?"

"It's Uncle Hiram, Nattie. He's in the hospital. It's his heart."

Hiram Moreland had hired Nattie for a receptionist's job at his detective agency when she was a twenty-year-old with two years of college. He encouraged her to become a PI, and he trusted her to manage his office. All of this occurred before his nephew, Nathan, came to the practice and swept her off her feet. *He had to sweep me off my feet,* she was fond of saying, *because I must have been unbalanced.*

"I'm on my way back to Bristol now," she told him. "I'll be at the hospital in twenty minutes."

"It's the Heart Center in Kingsport."

"Okay, I'll be there in forty minutes."

"Thanks, Nattie. I know he'll want to see you."

Even before she entered Hiram's hospital room, she could hear him telling the nurse he wanted to sit up higher. His heart procedure was a seven-hour ordeal in which they entered the ventricles through veins on either side of his groin. The first hours of recovery required him to lie flat so as to allow the veins to get a head start on healing. After that, the nurses would raise him fifteen degrees every hour. Hiram was arguing with the nurse about speeding up the process. It was good-natured, and it meant he was feeling his oats.

"Couldn't you have sutured his lips together when he was knocked out?" Nattie asked as she entered the room.

"We suggested that. They wouldn't do it." Angie, Hiram's wife, laughed. Hugging Nattie, she added, "It is good to see you, honey."

"Is he okay?" Nattie spoke in a whisper.

"Oh yeah," Angie made no effort to soften her voice. "This sounds more ominous than it is. He's fine, really. We will take him home tomorrow."

Nattie looked around Angie at Nathan, who was avoiding eye contact. *You better look the other way,* she thought.

Holding up a Pal's bag for Hiram to see, she stepped closer to his bed. "Look what I brought you, old man."

Hiram lit up like a child at Christmas. "A double cheese-burger," he chanted reaching for the bag.

"Oh no, is that what you wanted?" She pulled the bag from his reach. "I am so sorry. I must have forgotten what you liked. I got a foot-long Coney dog with chili."

"That will do," he said when she finally gave him her gift. His face lit up again as he retrieved the double cheeseburger from the bag. "Thank you."

"But I don't see how you could eat it while you are lying down like that. I'll just give it to Nathan." She reached for the cheeseburger.

"Pam," Hiram said to the nurse who had just entered the room, "would you throw him out of here?"

43

Pam looked at Hiram, who was shaking his finger at his nephew, and then glanced at Nathan. She rolled her eyes. "Let me check your cuts one more time before Sally gets here. She will be your night nurse."

Nattie put the bag with the rest of the food on the table next to Hiram. "Do you need me to go out in the hall?"

"Nah," answered Angie. She and Nattie watched Hiram take a bite from the Big Pal cheeseburger and grin. "Pam is very discrete."

While Hiram happily munched away, Pam stood on one side of him and pushed his sheet over just enough to take a look at the cut. Then she covered him up, circled the bed, and repeated the process from the other side. Angie was right, what Pam lacked in a sense of humor, she made up for in discretion.

"Thanks, Nattie," said Hiram, holding up half of the cheeseburger. "This is the best chili dog I have ever eaten."

Nattie smiled. "You're welcome, hi. Is there anything else I can do?"

With his mouth full from the next bite, he mumbled, "You can tell me about what you are working on these days."

"None of that now," Angie quickly interjected. "You are still in recovery. No business." Turning to Nattie, she repeated, "No business talk at all."

Nattie held her hands up in surrender.

Nathan finally joined in. "I am impressed, Aunt Angie. There aren't many people who can get Natasha McMorales to back down."

"She is not backing down, Junior," corrected Hiram. "She is retreating. Her mind is already plotting how to get around Angie and ask for advice from an old man."

"No, Hi, it was a straightforward retreat."

Just then Sally, the night nurse, came into the room and asked them to wait in the hall. Sally was of medium height, a sultry young redhead who could not have been a nurse more than a year or two at the most. "Would you all mind waiting in the hall for a moment?"

As Nathan followed Nattie into the hall, he whispered, "Why are you avoiding me?"

"I'm avoiding you? Is that why you made this sound more serious than it is? You nearly scared me out of my mind."

"How else–" Nathan did not finish his statement as Angie joined them in the hall.

From the hall they watched the Sally stand at the foot of Hiram's bed and lift the sheet up high enough to get a good look at his groin, "Are you feeling better?" Even her voice was sultry.

"He is now," said Angie under her breath.

CHAPTER 10

NATTIE'S FATHER CALLS

Nattie unlocked the front door of her home, entered, turned on the light, and hung her bag on the wall hook next to the door. Her keys went into a bowl on a little table next to the door. Originally the bowl held Halloween candy, but during the off-season it kept her keys where she could always find them. What she called her "cottage" was really an older Cape Cod, with a living room, kitchen, and dining room on the first floor and with two bedrooms on the second.

Closing the door behind her brought a feeling of safety. She liked her home. It was small, which made it cozy and needing less maintenance. The yard was just large enough to separate her from her neighbors but small enough to need less maintenance as well. The builder found it easier to leave the backyards alone, but leveled the trees in the front yards for easy access. This left two giant oak trees in the back and a single birch tree in the middle of the front yard.

Other landscaping in the front was simply the shrubs left by the previous owner who had told her they were low maintenance. "Low maintenance" were magic words for her as a first-time homeowner. The cottage was well built and simple to take care of. Most importantly, it represented a huge step into independence and adulthood. Leaving apartment life was a decision she made immediately after her divorce from Nathan. And here she was again, escaping from the confusion of Nathan's presence in her life by retreating to her cottage.

Her cottage was filled with wooden furniture and memorabilia from her grandparents' farm in Johnson City. If it were not for the pottery pieces scattered on tabletops around the room and the original artwork done by a college friend hanging on the walls the place would have looked like it was inhabited by a ninety-year-old. As it was, the furniture added another layer of depth to the "this is my home" effect.

It was an effect she looked forward to as she drove home from the hospital. It was good to see Hiram, but it was clear that his hospital stay was more of an excuse for Nathan to see her than a real emergency. She was extremely hungry and could have easily stopped on the way home; but had she slowed down, the thoughts of Nathan would have flooded her mind. So she kept moving, focusing her energy and attention on getting home, shutting off her phone, and making herself a late dinner. A late dinner meant she would be making breakfast: a cheese omelet, Ezekiel bread toast, and Café DuMonde decaf coffee.

After starting to heat water in the copper tea-kettle, she went upstairs to her bedroom and changed into a pair of sweat pants, an extra-large Chicago Bears jersey that had belonged to her father, and some fuzzy slippers that resembled Big Bird. She could hear the kettle whistling as she descended her staircase. Once her coffee was steeping in a small French press, she began to rummage in her refrigerator for ingredients to add to her omelet She decided on Roma tomatoes, green peppers, Anaheim chilies, and feta cheese and took them to the cutting board on the counter of the Hoosier Cabinet that was once her grandmother's. She set the Pandora application on her Blackberry phone on the Loreena McKinnett station and began to dice up her vegetables.

Nattie chopped her vegetables slowly, as her grandmother had taught her, and enjoyed the tranquility of the moment. Her grandmother had taught her how to make omelets, and they were the one thing she felt comfortable making without a recipe. There was no sense in second guessing her life, but it might be nice to have learned to cook more, or to have been more interested in learning from her grandmother when she could. *If a woman who doesn't cook is like a man who doesn't fix cars, then what does that make me?* mused Nattie as she munched on some cubes of green pepper.

It was a peaceful moment but it was gone all too quickly as her phone rang. She picked up the phone and looked at the screen. The call was from her father. For a moment she was tempted to ignore the call, but it was her father and he had probably just realized that her birthday was over a month ago.

"Hello, Daddy."

"Hey, Pumpkin. How are you?"

"I'm okay. What about you?"

He forced a laugh. "Oh, you know me."

Not really dad.

"I just got to missing my little girl and thought I'd give you a call."

"That's nice dad. It's good to hear from you." *Better late than never.* She had made a concerted effort to be more cordial with him over the last few years. Kevin told her that their father was sensitive to criticism and would retreat when he felt her disapproval. Although she felt completely justified in her attitude, she also realized how futile it was; so she determined herself to be cordial.

"Did you watch the Super Bowl this year?"

"Football?"

"Yeah, Pumpkin, football. Did you watch it this year?"

Nattie had to think about it. The Super Bowl was in January. That was six months ago. "I suppose I did. I usually watch it for the commercials, but that was half a year ago. I don't remember who played, much less who won."

"Who played was not as important as who played at halftime. It was the Who who played. Does that ring a bell?"

The Who who played—clever line, Dad. Is that why you called? She did not laugh.

"We always liked the Who," he reminisced.

By "we" you mean you liked them and I hung out with you.

"It was weird watching a bunch of sixty-year-old men singing 'Teenage Wasteland.'"

Nattie remembered. "That was weird."

He laughed and made another attempt to get her to laugh before saying goodbye, "it was the Who who wrote it, the Who who performed it, and the Who who shouldn't."

Nattie still did not laugh. It was a good line but all she could think about was her birthday last month.

The mood to cook was gone, but at least it left before she broke any eggs. The diced veggies fit nicely in an empty plastic container that a butter substitute had come in. She dumped the coffee down the sink and got a beer and a piece of cold pizza from the fridge. *I'll eat better tomorrow*, she promised herself as she headed towards the computer in the guest bedroom upstairs.

The computer room, as she called it, was a small bedroom. The room was dominated by an oversized desk, which left enough space for a single bed. It was in this room and this bed that she had brought Nathan to recuperate after he had been knocked unconscious when he attempted to protect her one night at his bar. He stayed in that room exactly one of the two nights he spent in her house. But the move to her bedroom was too fast and too much for her. He had not understood when she asked him to leave. "As far as I'm concerned we are still married," he had said. Until this evening she had not seen him since.

The phone call from her father had driven her thoughts of her ex-husband from her mind. She had put off writing about her father in her journal but the time seemed right. She began typing.

For all of my childhood my father was a functioning alcoholic. I didn't learn what that phrase meant until I was older, but that is what he was. He was a salesman and he was gone a lot. My mother said he could charm the money off anyone. I think she liked that he made a lot of money. She probably liked that he was charming too. He was very charming and generous and playful and funny. When he was in a good mood, he was everything you wanted a father to be. You just couldn't depend on his being in a good mood. It wasn't that he was ever mean or irritable when he was in a bad mood. He was never mean or irritable, ever. When he wasn't in a good mood he would simply be gone. It wouldn't matter if you needed him or if he had promised you something, he wouldn't be there. By the time I was ten, I didn't trust him anymore.

Kevin was six, so he still believed all the excuses when Dad's promises were broken. Mom seemed to be okay with it, too. In fact, Mom was the one who made the excuses for him. When I'd watch Kevin wait at the window for his father to show up, I'd tell him, "If Dad's late, it means he forgot." She'd tell me not to be so "sour," and then she'd make up some story about Dad working so hard or having such a hard job. And maybe she was right. Maybe I was sour, but I couldn't help seeing what I saw, knowing what I knew. I know he knew that I had turned sour towards him and sometimes I wonder if that made it worse when things got really bad.

Until I was eleven my father was a functioning alcoholic. Mostly he was happy. He was just irresponsible when it came to his family. At least I think he was happy. Everything changed after he got into that accident in Philadelphia. An eight year old girl named Martha stepped out in front of his car while he was looking for someone. It was early in the morning but he had already had a drink. His blood alcohol level was still legal, but who knows if it mattered? He did not see her. They arrested him and he had to go to court. His lawyer thought it would look better for him if his family were there, so mom went and she took me with her. She said she needed someone to lean on. I heard it all. I heard about his blood alcohol level, which was just barely legal but close enough to be mentioned. They asked about his drinking and I got to hear him lie. Martha's mother was at the hearing, and I got to hear her sobbing. And then when it was all over I got to hear what she called him, what she screamed at him as we left the courthouse. I don't know what that memory feels like to him, but I know what it feels like to me. After that he stopped being fun. He was home more than before, but when he was not being moody he was usually in bed. Six months later he was unemployed. And six months after that he and mom got divorced. She was no longer making excuses for him.

The pizza was long gone but the journal entry and the beer were timed to finish together. She stopped in the doorway and turned back to face her computer as if it were a person to whom she had been speaking. *Happy birthday*, she told herself as she turned of the light and headed to her bedroom.

CHAPTER 11

DEBBIE'S EAR

"It is complicated," explained Nattie across the lunch table at KP Duty.

Before Debbie could respond, the waitress came. Nattie ordered the endless soup and salad. It was Tuesday so the soup was tomato bisque and the house dressing tasted like Catalina with blue cheese crumbles. Her situation might have been complicated but ordering lunch was not.

Debbie ordered the same thing. When the waitress left she said, "I noticed you never look at a menu. At least you didn't look at a menu the two times we have eaten together."

"I guess I am a creature of habit," Nattie answered. "When I find what I like somewhere I usually order it. If I am eating lunch out on a Tuesday, then this is where I come."

Debbie nodded. "I am glad you were free for lunch when I called this morning. Being new in town, I don't know anyone yet."

"I'm glad you called."

"Me too. You were saying it's complicated when I asked about your relationship status."

Nattie tried not to flinch. Getting up close and personal was not a comfortable activity for her. Experience had taught her that there were two kinds of men in the world: those you could not count on because they were immature and those you could not count on because they were self-serving users.

Nattie knew the world was more complicated than that, and she also knew her thinking was unfair and even self-defeating; but it also kept her safe from disappointment. The lone-wolf strategy was getting tiresome, though, so she had determined to begin opening up to someone. And while the complications of the last twenty-four hours swimming in her head, Debbie had called. *Debbie could be a gift from heaven,* thought Nattie after they made their lunch date, *or she could be the bait in a trap with my name on it.*

She thought about telling Debbie about the phone call from officer Alan Poe on her answering machine. The call was waiting for her when she got to her office that morning. Alan was a nice guy—attractive, fit, and responsible—and, strangely enough, the fact that she had once been very nasty to him made his kindness to her now even more intriguing. His message simply told her she could call him if she needed any help with her investigation. She called back and told his answering machine that she appreciated his offer and would be taking him up on it soon. It was all very innocent, so it alarmed her to realize that she was nervous as she returned his call. Having no idea how to talk about Alan Poe made the decision not to talk about him easy.

"The short version is this," began Nattie. "I wasn't married very long before my husband's alcohol abuse got intolerable. One broken promise after another finally got the best of me and I called it quits."

"Sometimes you have to draw a line. And it doesn't help if you still love him."

Nattie eyed her. "No it doesn't."

"Do you still love him?"

"Probably," Nattie admitted, surprising herself. "But I cannot go there. Not yet."

"Is he sober now?"

Shrugging, Nattie answered, "Maybe. He says he's sober. But he owns a bar."

"That is a red flag."

"And he hasn't really changed, either. If I let him get close, I end up taking care of him. If I keep my distance, he tries to navigate his way around my boundaries. Just last night he got me to visit his uncle at the hospital by letting me believe his uncle was in serious trouble."

"Let me guess. He was there when you got there."

Nattie nodded.

"So you love him, but can't live with him. You can't let him in, but you can't keep him away, either."

"That sums it up nicely," observed Nattie.

"So how do you handle it?"

"I stay as busy as I can."

CHAPTER 12

STATE STREET

After her lunch with Debbie, Nattie walked back up State Street to her office. There was no hurry to get back. The Gil Peters case was the only piece of business at the moment and there was nothing to tend to regarding that case until it was time to go interview the bartender who may have been one of the last people to see Norris Trainor alive. As Kevin had the office covered she decided to walk leisurely.

Peace and goodwill, she said, reminding herself of Saint Francis and his view of simplifying life. She focused her energy and attention on breathing deeply and enjoying the familiar sights.

Stopping to watch some men working on the exterior of a new business going in on the Virginia side of the street, she read the sign in the window, "Sessions 27." As she stood wondering what Sessions 27 meant, a man she did not recognize passed her wearing a yellow Hawaiian shirt. A smile crossed her face as she watched the stranger continue down the street. Nathan had a similar yellow Hawaiian shirt. It was, in fact his favorite shirt when they were first married. The sight brought one of the more pleasant memories of their marriage. They had been married for only eight months when he returned from a business trip to Indianapolis. He went there to call on the Dakota Insurance

Company's claim center on behalf of the Hiram Moreland Detective Agency where he and she both worked. He was in the shower when Nattie began unpacking his suitcase. He emerged, half wet, from the bathroom as she lifted his favorite shirt, the yellow Hawaiian. It had been wadded up and shoved into the case. As she held it out for inspection she asked him, "Can you explain how all these cockle burrs got stuck on your shirt while you were calling on an insurance company?" She guessed there may have been twenty-five or thirty cockle burrs, but it was not the quantity that needed explaining as much as the placement. The cockle burrs were stuck to the inside of his shirt.

Nathan had gotten friendly with a couple of claims managers while he was in Indianapolis during the day and they invited him out for dinner that evening. They had worked late into evening and it was after 9:30 when they picked him up at the Holiday Inn. They went to a Mexican place and he had a beer with the chips and salsa. He quickly ordered another beer when he discovered that his entree was hotter than he expected. One of the men ordered after dinner drinks for the table. The most Nattie had ever seen him drink was two beers or two glasses of wine so she knew he was already past his comfort zone.

After dinner they went somewhere else for dessert but the place they went only served drinks. Nattie knew he was describing a strip club but she did not let him know that she knew. After several Navy Grogs they started to take him back to his motel on the west side of Indianapolis. Nathan was unable to hide his inebriated state from his hosts who thought it would be funny to describe going out to breakfast and getting some greasy fried eggs. After hearing the phrase "greasy fried eggs" one too many times Nathan tried franticly to roll down his window. He just barely got it rolled down as far as it would go before he lost control of the contents of their evening's entertainment. Unfortunately for them all, Nathan did not realize that the windows in the rear doors of most cars only go down half way. In an effort to minimize the damage of his miscalculation Nathan tried to clean up as much as he could with his shirt. He was too drunk to throw up through the open portion of his window but not too drunk to take care of his favorite Hawaiian shirt which he removed, set aside, and then used his white tee shirt as a rag/mop.

Once they got to the Holiday Inn parking lot the driver got some rags and a bottle of windshield wiper fluid to finish the cleanup job Nathan had started with his undershirt while Nathan stood bare-chested and held his precious yellow Hawaiian shirt in his hands. All was well until they heard a screech of tires and a collision from Interstate 465 bypass behind the motel. They could not see the accident because there was a large field and a dip between the parking lot and the highway. Nathan was the last to sprint towards the accident because he took the time to put his shirt on, not noticing that it was inside out. Being a former baseball player and the youngest of the three, "helper" Nathan quickly outran his hosts and was the first one to reach the wire fence that bordered the highway. He did not see the fence until he hit it full speed.

Nattie's smile crept into a full giggle as she watched the stranger in the yellow shirt disappear into the Paramount Theater. She could giggle because it was funny. This, of course was before his alcoholism had kicked in, so she had not been alarmed by the story at the time. Even now it was the funny to picture her athletic husband sprinting bare-chested with an inside out shirt flying behind him as he outraced his friends across a dark field and blindly hitting that waist high fence. She could still picture him flipping over the fence and landing on his back. Another image, one she got to see frequently, was the expression on his face when she held up that shirt with the cockle burrs inside it. He looked at the shirt and then looked at her with the kind of "who me?" crooked smiles little boys use to get out of trouble. *I guess I am one of those women who likes for men to have a little bit of little boy inside of them. But, like most women, I could not wait forever for a little boy to grow up.*

A different mood came over her as she resumed her walk back to her office. The spontaneity, the playfulness, the childlike-ness were all memories that were fond at the time and fondly remembered, but remembering them would also morph into sadness and regret. This awareness brought an unwanted realization; *this is exactly what happens when I remember fun times with my father.*

CHAPTER 13

BEE HEAVEN

Get busy, she told herself as she entered the office. When a computer gets stuck you re-boot by turning it off for a while, but when a mind gets stuck on something negative it cannot simply be turned off. Re-booting a mind that is dwelling on negativity has to be done by changing the focus, much like changing the channel on a television set. Nattie could not remember which self-help book she learned this strategy from, but she remembered the technique. Repeated use is a great aid to remembering.

"Look at this," said Kevin from behind his computer.

Nattie could feel her shoulders tighten. The last thing she wanted at that moment was to get drawn into whatever Kevin's fascination du jour was. Instead of circling the counter where she could look at what was on his computer screen, she stepped up to the counter in front of his desk.

Leaning against the counter, "Any calls?"

"Camden Stark called again."

"How is he?"

"Same old stuff."

"Who is after him this time?"

"CIA again."

Camden Stark was an eccentric older gentleman who wrote letters to the editor fairly often. Mostly he proposed changes to the Federal

57

Government. His last letter proposed that we abolish the election procedure and remodel it after the Miss America pageant. 'We do not know these people we are voting for, we only know what the media tells us, and we do not know them either.' His suggestion was that we only elect local officials, and we send them to a conference where those there elect county officials. The county officials in turn are sent to the state where they elect state officials from amongst themselves. State officials get together and from amongst themselves they elect federal officials. That way every level in the hierarchy will be filled by someone who rose to the top of the next level down, elected by the people of that level who at least had first hand experience of everyone at that level of the hierarchy.

Nattie remembered reading his letter and immediately thinking it was insane, but then after reflecting it began to make more and more sense, only to eventually be deemed insane again.

Normally when Camden called it was because he was convinced that some branch of the federal government had been so threatened by his ideas that they were plotting ways to shut him up. The calls dated back to when it was Hiram Moreland Detective Agency. Hiram had investigated an early complaint but had quickly returned Camden's money. 'We aren't in the business of taking money from paranoids,' was Hiram's response. Hiram did not say that to Camden however, he said it to Nattie just before he told her to handle it. That was when Nattie was the receptionist. Kevin was the receptionist now.

"Can you handle it?"

"I tried sis. He says he wants to talk to you."

Of course he wants to talk to me. And I want you to handle it. "Give me the phone number."

Handing her a pink slip of paper with Camden's phone message on it, "Here you go, but you don't have to call him now, I told him you would be heading out to Barley Corners this afternoon and that your schedule was completely full tomorrow."

"Why Kevin, you stalled him."

"I did," he agreed without smiling, "he is always much easier to deal with when he can get a few days past the first wave of paranoia."

"Very clever, Kevin. I'd call that handling it, thanks."

Shrugging, "You're welcome, but you will still have to call him eventually."

"Maybe we should offer him his own parking place."

"I think you should offer him a job."

Nattie stepped back from the counter. With wide-open eyes, "Offer him a job? Are you serious? He would drive us crazy."

"Maybe, but maybe his natural born suspiciousness would make him a pretty good detective."

Stepping back up to the counter Nattie squinted at him.

"Seriously sis, if he had all that craziness focused on something productive he could be amazing."

"Why don't I offer him your job?"

Without looking up from the computer screen Kevin answered, "Oh he would drive you nuts if he had my job. Not enough stimulation to keep him busy." He looked up and smiled, "My job requires a highly developed ability to manage idle time."

A highly developed ability to manage idle time, which will look impressive on your resume. "Is that a skill you have?"

Kevin did not answer.

That may have been the dumbest question I have ever asked. "I withdraw the question," a mock bow, "You may be the prince of managing idle time. Tell me, your majesty, how have you managed your idle time today?" As soon as she had asked her question she realized, *no, that is the dumbest question I have ever asked.*

"Come around here and look."

Lord, help me, she prayed as she circled the counter.

On the computer screen, in large letters, was the phrase; "AIN'T MISS BEE HEAVEN"

"Ain't miss bee heaven …. Ain't misbehavin'" she looked at him for a clue to what it might mean.

Kevin's smile grew, as if expecting her to figure something out any moment.

"I give up Kevin. What does it mean?"

"It's an advertising slogan."

Nattie nodded. Looking back at the computer screen, "A slogan for what?"

Sitting back in his chair and spreading his hands apart, "Imagine a honey farm."

"A honey farm?"

"A farm with a lot of pastures and a lot of bee hives."

"Okay."

"And we'd call it 'Bee Heaven.'"

"We?"

"We. Me. Us. It doesn't matter who right now. Just picture the Bee heaven."

"Where you will keep bees and process honey."

"Yes! And also where we will have visitors come. Maybe tourists. Maybe parents will bring their kids for the educational tours of the hives and the processing barn. Maybe it will be people who just want to eat in the Honey Moon Dining Room, where honey is the featured ingredient on the menu."

"Honey glazed ham sandwiches?"

"Oh I am sure we could do much better than that. But we can figure that out later." Pointing at the slogan, "When our visitors leave we will give them each a button with that slogan on it."

"Ain't miss bee heaven," she read out loud again, "Shouldn't it read, 'I went to Bee Heaven,' or 'I didn't miss Bee Heaven'?"

"'Ain't misbehaving' is an old song."

"Yes, a very old song."

"Yes, but a very good, very old song. And we could play that on our website and in the dining room and when it caught on again it would be associated with us," the new insight made Kevin beamed excitedly.

"I don't want to bust your bubble Kev, but do you know anything about bees? Or honey?" *Or finishing anything you start?*

"Not yet," he replied, "but I will. I can learn all I need to learn with all my …"

"idle time," they said in unison finishing his sentence.

Kevin slowed down his laughter before Nattie. Looking at his watch, "Shouldn't you be heading out to Barley Corners about now?"

Nattie saluted, "I'll get out of the way of your research your majesty."

As she reached the door she hesitated. There was something odd in the way he said, 'have a good trip,' but she did not think about it for long.

CHAPTER 14

THE NEVER TELL TAVERN

Nathan Moreland was waiting in the parking lot when Nattie left her office. As their eyes meet he quickly straightened up from where he had been leaning on the door of her Subaru. "Nat," he said tentatively.

"Nate," she replied. It was a greeting they had played with for most of their relationship. 'Nat and Nate and all the cuteness you could hate' was the slogan for their imaginary reality show. Normally it was said in a playful spirit, but this time her reply was not playful at all.

Taking her reflexive response as permission to be playful he announced, "I got shotgun," as he walked around to the passenger side of the car.

"Nate, I am working."

"I know."

"No really," she pressed on. "I am heading out to Barley Corners."

"Yeah, I know. To The Never Say Never Bar and Grill. I want to hitch a ride out there. I heard it was a real nice place, and I want to see it for myself."

"Maybe to pick up an idea or two for Our House?" Our House was the name of Nathan's bar. His alcoholism had played a big part in the ruin of their marriage, so his purchase of a bar after their divorce did not help his attempt at reconciliation.

"Yeah."

She eyed him across the top of her Subaru Forester. "Really, Nate? You have heard that this Never Say Never place is real nice?"

He eyed her back. "You do not look like you believe me, Nat." After a moment of studying her face, "Did I goof up the name?"

She nodded.

He rolled his eyes. "It figures." It was more an existential statement than a response to her. "What is the name anyway?"

"The Never Tell Tavern."

"Dang," he joked as he pretended to pound his right fist on the roof of her car. "You have to admit I was close."

Leaning further across her car, she asked, "What is this all about, Nathan?" The use of his full name made it clear that the playfulness was not being encouraged.

"I just wanted some time for us to talk. I tried to set up an appointment through Kevin." Spreading his arms out across the roof of her car, "This is what I got."

It figures, she thought existentially. She already knew that it was 2 o'clock, but looking at her watch bought a bit of time to think. "If you go with out me to Barley Corners I can not guarantee I will have you back in Bristol until 6 o'clock at the earliest."

"I'm in." He patted the roof and got into the passenger seat.

She got in too.

Laughing heartily, "Just think of me as your bodyguard."

Nattie smiled, but did not laugh. His bodyguard joke was at his own expense. It referenced an incident in his bar when he was knocked unconscious in an attempt to protect her from a very large, very scary looking man. Nattie had taken tender care of him immediately after she broke the scary man's nose.

Following the bartender's directions, Nattie drove through town and wove her way along the river until she found the gravel parking lot of the tavern. The drive to Barley Corners had taken close to an hour and a half with a quick drive-thru at a McDonalds in Kingsport for coffee. If Nathan was going to initiate a serious conversation, then apparently it was going to take place on the way back.

You could never tell the Never Tell was a tavern if it were not for the sign. It looked more like a bait house and probably was when it was first built, which was longer ago than Nattie could imagine.

"Get any good ideas for your place yet?" she said under her breath as Nate held the screen door open for her.

"The screen door is a nice touch," he said, following her through.

They stood just inside the door and surveyed the room. It was nothing like the outside. Overhead fans created a nice breeze throughout the room, which was dominated by oak tables and chairs, a bar covered with white drop cloths, and what looked like walnut paneling. The cabinets behind the bar were cherry. Other than the bar itself, the room looked like it could have been the game room in an exclusive men's club in a downtown business district of an old city like Philadelphia or Boston.

Where am I? wondered Nattie.

"Wanna beer?" asked a very large man who had been kneeling behind the bar. His thinning hair was pulled back into a ponytail, and his beard was neatly trimmed.

Cajun? Nattie tried to guess the accent. "Diet coke?"

"Rum?"

"Just the diet coke, thanks. I am Nattie Moreland. Are you Mr. Robinette?"

"Yep," he said. "Beauregard Boo. That is Boo, like from *To Kill a Mockingbird*, Robinette. Are you the detective from Bristol?"

"I am," Nattie said as she sat at the bar.

"Beer?" Beauregard Boo Robinette asked Nathan.

Nathan took the stool next to Nattie. "Got any coffee?"

Beauregard put a toothpick in the corner of his mouth and answered, "We got great coffee. I grind it myself. It's got chicory and a few other secrets in it." He took out the toothpick and pointed it at Nathan. "I'll tell you what. If you don't like it I won't charge you."

"It is a deal," answered Nathan. "Are you the owner?"

Beauregard nodded, "And the cook, carpenter, and bartender too."

"This place looks fantastic, doesn't it Nattie?"

Nattie nodded enthusiastically.

"It's coming along."

"Are you doing the work yourself?"

"I am. I'm glad you like it. When I finish the outside it will be for sale."

Nattie watched Nathan take another slow scan around the room. She knew what he was thinking. While Nattie watched Nathan dream about the possibilities, Beauregard got their drinks.

Nathan took a sip of the coffee. "Oh wow," he said slowly, "that is good. I don't suppose you would tell me what else is in it?"

"Nothing illegal, if that concerns you. And if you buy the place, I will tell you all the secrets."

"You've got other secrets?" asked Nattie.

Beauregard grinned and spread his arms out. "This place was a dump when I got it a year ago. My aunt ran a bait and tackle shop here, and I got it when she passed. It never made any money so I decided to turn it into a bar. I got the idea from those house flipping shows on television. So I'm flipping this bait shop into a tavern."

"How's business?"

"I don't get much business during the day, but that gives me time to work on the building. The drinkers will start showing up in an hour or so." He threw the toothpick away. "I get anywhere from ten to twenty on most week nights; but I cook on the weekend, and this place packs out. When I am done remodeling, I will cook all week and then this place will take off— That's the plan anyway."

"What's your specialty?"

"Red beans and rice is the big seller. Folks around here like that as a side to their hamburgers and steaks. But the Jambalaya is gonna catch on."

"I thought you might be from New Orleans," observed Nattie. "Were you a chef there?"

"I've done a little of everything in my life. But before Katrina hit New Orleans, I was a therapist."

"Really!" Nathan blurted out.

Beauregard chuckled, "I know. I don't exactly look like it, but that is what I did for twenty-five years. After Katrina, a managed-care company took over the agency I worked for, and it was not a job I wanted anymore. When this opportunity came along, I saw it as my way out."

"Are you going to go back to New Orleans when you sell this place?"

"Probably not. In New Orleans everyone sounds like me and I am just an okay cook. But here I am a novelty and my food is unique. Besides, I think I can do better therapy from behind this bar than I could when I was working for accountants. Do either of you need refills?"

"I'm fine," said Nattie. Nathan held out his cup.

While Beauregard poured more coffee for Nathan, he addressed Nattie, "If I can't sell this guy my place, then you might as well go ahead and ask me about that night."

Nattie took photos of Norris Trainor and Gil Peters from her bag and placed them on the bar, "Do you recognize these men?"

"Of course." He tapped on the picture of Norris. "That is the guy that got killed in my parking lot."

"And the other man?"

"They were here together, then he left. This one," he added, pointing at Norris again, "stayed for another beer."

"What can you tell me about the way they were?"

Beauregard looked confused.

"Did you notice anything unusual about the way they interacted? Did they argue?"

"Oh mercy, no. They were really enjoying themselves. I had a cold one myself with them. They talked about buying this place together, but they weren't serious about it."

"Did you tell that to the police when they interviewed you?"

Confusion once again crossed Beauregard's face. "I thought this was the police interview. You said you were a detective from Bristol."

"Private detective. I work for the family of the man accused of the murder. I am sorry for the confusion, but I thought I was following up on the police investigation."

"The only investigation with me was the next day an officer came here and showed me pictures of these two guys and asked me if they were here that night. I said yes and that was it. I guess if they caught the guy already they would not be too concerned with what I have to say."

Tapping the photo of Gil Peters, Nattie asked, "What would you say if I told you this is the accused?"

He bent over the photos to take another look. "Seriously?"

"He was arrested the next day."

65

Beauregard scratched his head. "I suppose he could have done; but if he did, then he is one serious sociopath."

"We are not counselors Mr. Robinette. Could you explain what you mean by that?"

"No jargon please," added Nathan.

"I would have bet anything that those two guys were really good friends. When I retired as a therapist, I figured I had over 30,000 hours of working intimately with people. And I also would have bet anything that neither of them could have been a killer. It would have taken a cold-blooded liar to be able to fool an experienced therapist that much. So—" He flipped his thumb over at Gil's picture on the bar. "If he did it, he is a cold-blooded liar with no feeling of guilt or remorse."

They drove in silence for the first half hour. Nathan allowed Nattie the quiet to think about what she heard and what she would do next. He was not able to pull into himself and reflect the way she could, the way she needed to. It was one of the qualities that mystified him about her. At least he knew enough to be quiet and stay out of her way.

"Did you get the ideas you were hoping for by going with me?" she finally asked as they passed Kingsport.

"Well, besides installing a screen door, I did think about adding a unique food item to the menu; but I don't know what it could be. I could not pull off Cajun like he does. I'll have to think about it. How about you? Did you get what you wanted?"

"Maybe. Just because a psychotherapist thinks my client could not be a killer is not proof of anything. But it does help me decide whether or not I believe him."

"And?"

"And my client is no sociopath. I wondered if he might have done it in a panic or a rage; but after talking to Beauregard, I don't think that was it, either. I think someone else did it."

Nate realized that it was no longer he she was speaking to. He was listening to her talk herself through the maze she found herself in.

"Nat," he said very seriously, "if I was accused of something I did not do, I would sure want you in my corner. I don't know if your client appreciates it yet, but I know that he could not be in better hands than yours."

She looked at him for a moment. "Thank you, Nathan. That was very nice to hear."

"It is the truth."

"So what did you want to talk to me about?"

"I wanted to talk about the weekend we spent together."

Nattie shifted in her seat and focused on the road in front of her.

"You took real good care of me after that guy almost broke my jaw. I mean it, Nat; you were great to me. And I thought after what happened—"

She cut him off. "We were married, Nate. We still care about each other. It was a strange situation, and we comforted each other. I don't think we should make a bigger deal out of it than that."

"It was a big deal to me. I thought we could see where things between us could go."

"We know where things between us go."

"It could be different this time. I have not had a drink in eleven months."

"I am glad about that, Nate; I really am. But eleven months is not long enough for me. I can not say it will never happen, but it can not happen now."

"So you avoided me for two months."

"I am sorry that it seemed like I was avoiding you. I have been busy with the agency." Her hands tightened on the steering wheel. "No, that is not the truth. I was avoiding you. I was scared. What happened that weekend should not have happened. It cannot happen again."

It was his turn to stare forward.

She touched his left arm tenderly. "I do not want to hurt you, Nate, but I don't think you should wait for me either."

Turning abruptly towards her, he said, "That is just it. That is what I came to tell you."

"What?"

"I can't just wait for you to trust me, Nattie."

"What are you saying?"

"I am saying that I have started seeing someone."

The news jolted her. There was another woman in his life. She had not considered that he could be with another woman. Now that she considered it, it surprised her that it had never occurred to her. She had no idea what she felt. Anger? Maybe. Fear? A bit. Confusion, at least. Shock? Absolutely. Without knowing what to do, she did what she always did.

"That is great. I am happy for you, Nate. Tell me about her. Is she nice?"

"Her name is Randi Lester, and we have only gone out twice. It is no big thing. I just wanted to tell you myself."

"That is completely unnecessary," she told him, but thought, *you better not let me hear it from someone else.* "Where did you meet? The bar?"

"No. Glen Frankle invited me over for dinner and Randi was there too," he lied. He had met her at his friend's house, but he had met her at his bar first.

"Glen fixed you up then." *Thanks Glen.*

"Are you okay with this?"

No I'm not okay you dunce. "Look, Nate, we are not married. You are free to go out with someone if you want to. I am not your wife. You do not owe me an explanation, and you do not need permission from me." *Then why am I reacting this way? This is too much. I am acting like a lunatic. I have no right to feel this way. What am I feeling anyway? Get a grip Nattie. Get a grip in a hurry.*

Without noticing her knuckles turning white as she gripped the steering wheel, "Can you believe that bartender's name?"

"Beauregard Boo?"

"Yeah. What do you think the other kindergarteners called him—Beau-Beau or boo-boo?"

CHAPTER 15

NATTIE REACTS TO NATHAN

"Debbie?"

"Yes," came Debbie's voice over the phone.

"This is Nattie."

"Hi Nattie. Do you need directions?" asked Debbie. She had invited Nattie to come for dinner and to meet her husband, Duane.

"No," she said. "I'm afraid I'm going to have to bail out on you. I know it is short notice."

"That's okay, Nattie. We were having lasagna and it keeps in the fridge just fine. Are you okay? You don't sound like yourself. Are you sick?"

"I do feel like I'm coming down with something." *Heart-sickness with cold chills and chronic confusion.*

"Can I do anything? I have a can of chicken soup in the cupboard. I could bring that by in a half hour."

"That is very nice of you, Debbie, but I think I just need to put on my pajamas and take the rest of the night off. I have something in my freezer that is ready to go."

"Is it healthy?"

"It's just what I need at the moment. Thanks for being so understanding."

69

"No problem. Call me if you need anything."
"I will and I'll take a rain-check on that dinner."
"Just name the time. And you take care of yourself."
"I am."

After hanging up, Nattie put on her pajamas, put *Pride and Prejudice* into her DVD player, and went to the freezer for the half gallon of Moose Tracks ice cream she bought after she dropped Nathan off at his bar.

CHAPTER 16

SKINNER, O'BRIEN, & WATSON

Nattie did not expect the ambush. Her phone conversation with Greg Taylor, Callie Trainor's lawyer, had gone as well as could be expected. He explained how much Mrs. Trainor wanted to avoid any conversations about her husband's murder, and Nattie had explained how little that was possible.

"The current investigation will expand," Nattie told him. "When Mr. Peters lawyers up Mrs. Trainor will not be able to avoid these conversations. Eventually she will have to talk to me."

Greg Taylor finally agreed to the meeting after Nattie pointed out that calling him first rather than just showing up at her house was a courtesy and a demonstration of her commitment to respecting the boundaries of everyone concerned. To further demonstrate this commitment, she agreed to meet at the lawyer's office.

As was her custom, Nattie arrived at the offices of Skinner, O'Brien, and Watson fifteen minutes early. Fox News was on in the waiting room, but she preferred to read. She took a copy of *Murder Takes the Cake* by Gayle Trent out of her bag and made herself comfortable.

"They will see you now," said a young woman with a pleasant voice.

I bet you did not know that my mother had your job a decade ago, thought Nattie as she followed the young woman down a hallway towards the conference room. She could have found it herself, but there was nothing to be gained in making that point.

Occupying the middle of the conference room was a large wooden table surrounded by what might have been twenty upholstered chairs. The door opened to the middle of the room. The arrangement could create several different effects depending upon what effect was needed. Men with solemn expressions facing the door was intended to make one feel as if he were approaching a panel of judges. The same group of men sitting with their backs to the door could make one feel marginalized.

Nattie expected to find Greg Taylor at one end of the table with Callie Trainor sitting next to him. She expected them to be at the left end of the table because that is where the hospitality bar was located. What she found when she entered was Greg Taylor sitting alone on the far side of the table facing the door. He had his lawyer uniform on: dark gray suit, white shirt, and purple striped tie. He stood when she entered the room and smiled warmly as he buttoned his jacket.

"Is Mrs. Trainor running late?" asked Nattie.

"Hello, Natalie."

She recognized the voice all too well. It was Lionel O'Brien, her stepfather, who was pouring a cup of coffee.

"Please," he said as he came to stand near her, "have a seat."

As Nattie sat down, he placed the cup of coffee in front of her, "Black with sugar, right?"

"Actually, it is black with Splenda; but nothing for me at the moment, thank you. I did not expect to see you today."

He patted her on the shoulder. "We like to be pretty informal around here. You knew that. I am just here getting myself a cup of coffee." He removed the coffee from in front of Nattie. "Can I get you something else? Water? A soda?"

"No nothing, thank you. I am fine," she answered while wondering, *What is going on here and where is my appointment? Lionel O'Brien's presence is not a good sign, but what does it mean?* She knew he had a personal assistant who got his coffee for him on the second floor where the three partners had their offices.

He turned his attention across the table. Motioning for Greg Taylor to sit, he asked, "How about you, Greg? Coffee?"

"No thank you Mr. O'Bri— Lionel."

Apparently, Greg Taylor did not get the memo about being informal around here either.

"Well," Lionel said, "I might as well take this cup, then."

You might as well, Nattie said to herself. *You made it the way you like it anyway.*

As he made his way back to the hospitality bar, Nattie turned to face Greg Taylor. "Is Mrs. Trainor on her way?"

"Not exactly," he half whined.

"Please do not tell me that for the second time in three days my appointment to see her—made in good faith, mind you—is getting road-blocked?"

"Look, Ms Moreland," he said, using his soothing voice, "we appreciate that you are just doing your job, but you have to appreciate that we are doing our job as well."

Nattie glanced at her stepfather. He was busy with something on the counter and did not appear to be listening. Nattie knew that he was listening and that the "we" Greg had referred to was he. Until she knew what the power play was all about, she would pretend that she did not notice it.

"Mrs. Trainor has decided to decline invitations to meet with you. It is her right to do so, and we would appreciate it if you would respect that."

"As I told you on the phone, Mr. Taylor, this is ludicrous. When Gil Peters hires himself an attorney, she will surely be subpoenaed. She will have to talk to me then."

He spread his hands. "She will have to talk to someone, but it does not have to be you, Ms Moreland."

Nattie could not believe her ears. "Excuse me. Was that a threat?"

"We would prefer to keep this amiable. If, however, you do not respect Mrs. Trainor's wishes, then she will be forced to file a restraining order against you."

"Now, now," said Lionel, who was suddenly hovering over Nattie. "I am sure that it will not come to that. I know that Natalie does her job in a most ethical manner. We do not need to resort to threats."

But it did not stop you.

73

"I am sure she understands the sensitive nature of this matter." Turning to Nattie, he explained, "The Trainor woman just lost her husband. I know you will respect how distraught she must be. Letting her have this time of grief is the Christian thing to do."

When she was in high school, the phrase "the Christian thing to do" always meant his preferences, not hers—music *he* wanted her to turn off or clothing *he* wanted her not to wear.

He rested his hand on her shoulder and smiled a comforting smile that he had surely practiced in a mirror. "Please do not take this so personally. Her refusal to speak to you again was not, I am sure, because you did anything wrong. You probably caught her at just the wrong time."

"Personally?" asked Nattie. "How can I take it personally? I have never met her."

Lionel flinched slightly and glanced momentarily at his young lawyer. His confusion lasted only a moment before he composed himself, but the moment did not go unnoticed by Nattie.

"Listen, Natalie. I think Alan Borland just got a case this morning that could really use a good PI. Could I put in a good word for you?"

Nattie smiled, "I could use all the good words I can get."

He nodded. "Good; that is settled. And I think we are on this Sunday for lunch, are we not?"

"We are."

"Good," he said. "See you then."

When Lionel was clear of the room, Nattie stood to leave.

Greg spoke. "Do we understand each other about the Trainor case?"

"I understand," said Nattie. *I understand that she does not want this investigation to involve her, and I understand that you lied to your boss about my meeting her once. I do not understand why though, ... but I will.*

CHAPTER 17

NATTIE FOLLOWS CALLIE TO THERAPY

Nattie hated boredom as much as she hated anything. The thought of simply waiting was near to torture for her. She often wondered if she had ADD or a type-A personality. *Maybe? She* laughed to herself. *Guard your heart, girlfriend, for you are the Queen of type-A personality.*

Unfortunately for Nattie, her career required surveillance, and that often meant sitting in a car waiting for something to happen. An easy solution would be to listen to music or, better yet, a book on tape. Hiram, her mentor, once caught her listening to the radio while on a stake-out and, after sneaking up on her, startled her so severely that she thought she was having a heart attack.

"Sorry to scare you," he had said without a trace of sorrow in his expression. "But you need to learn that your ears are sometimes more important than your eyes."

Hiram was right. She did need to learn that and never again listened to anything other than a police scanner, and that occasionally, while on surveillance. It was not the last time someone caught her off guard from behind, but even that was getting better. Sometimes, she would read, but that was only because she had taught herself to split her attention between a book and something else.

The reading strategy did not always work, of course. When this aspect of her job was required at night, as it more often than not did, her type-A personality got especially ramped up. "All-nighters" is what she called them. How she fought off going stir crazy during an all-nighter was a strategy she acquired from Spencer, Robert Parker's fictional detective. When Spencer was on an all-nighter, he would imagine all-star baseball teams. For instance, one night he listed the best first baseman he had ever personally seen play, then second base, short-stop, and so on. Another night he made up another all-star line up, but used only players of Italian descent.

Spencer's strategy needed to be adapted, for Nattie knew nothing about baseball. Her family was all Chicago Cubs fans, so that was no help. Nattie's adaptation called for top-ten lists. The top-ten list of the last all-nighter was a ranking of her favorite places to eat breakfast. Tonight's all-nighter had her parked down the street from Callie Trainor's home, and the top-ten list was favorite romantic comedies. The night provided no sightings of the elusive Callie Trainor, but she finished her list. With a three-way tie for first place and two honorable mentions, her list was as follows:

1. *Sweet Home Alabama*
2. *French Kiss*
3. *Knotting Hill*
4. *America's Sweethearts*
5. *My Big Fat Greek Wedding*
6. *House sitter*
7. *Roxanne*
8. *When Harry Met Sally*
9. *Overboard*
10. *The Bounty Hunter* (although she hadn't actually seen this movie, it made the list by virtue of the trailers)

Honorable mentions:
1. *Fools Rush In* (This movie didn't make her laugh so much. It made the list, however, because it has the greatest movie line said by a guy, "You are everything I never knew I always wanted")

2. *Milk Money* (Like *Fools Rush In*, this movie made the list because of a great line, the one delivered by Melanie Griffin, who tells a prepubescent boy, "Yes, there is a place on a woman's body that if a guy touches it, she will do whatever he wants. It's her heart.")

At 9:30 a.m. the Trainor garage door opened, and a cranberry-colored Honda Accord backed out. A woman, presumably Callie Trainor, got out of the car and closed the garage door. She was blonde and slender, and dressed casually, with running shoes, khaki shorts, a white golf shirt, and dark sunglasses. She had one of those figures that made clothing from Old Navy look expensive. Nattie snapped several pictures of her.

Callie got back into her car and drove to Bristol, with Nattie following at a discreet distance. The red Honda entered an older residential neighborhood, one which was unfamiliar to Nattie, and finally turned into the driveway of a small Cape Cod home. The sign out front read, "CHARLOTTE STEVENS, MA, LMFT."

Nattie drove down the street, turned around, and parked. So far, Callie Trainor had shown no signs that she was aware of being followed. While Nattie waited, she called Kevin and asked him to Google MA and LMFT because she did not know what the letters meant.

"What was your major in college again?" he asked.

"Psychology, why?"

"Because MA means she has a Master of Arts degree and LMFT stand for Licensed Marriage and Family—"

"Therapist." Nattie finished his sentence.

"Yes. I thought a psych major would have known that."

"I was probably sick that day," she responded. "And Kevin."

"Yes."

"You sounded like Mom just then."

"Ouch," he said and hung up.

Nattie reasoned that if Callie were seeing a therapist, it would be an hour before she came out. This gave her time to make a run for coffee and decide what her next move would be.

Instead of an hour, Callie came out after only forty-five minutes, startling Nattie enough to spill her coffee across her front seat. She still had not made a decision, but Callie's u-turn on her way to her car gave Nattie a little more time to decide what she was going to do.

The decision came in a flash. She drove her car into the driveway and parked next to Callie's Honda. By the time she exited her Subaru, Callie was returning to the driveway. Up close, Callie Trainor was beautiful. Too slender to be considered voluptuous, but beautiful nonetheless. She looked like Nattie's father's favorite actress, Grace Kelly. Despite her attractiveness, however, Callie's expression was sullen. The Peters had called her aloof, which accurately described her behavior just now. She unlocked her car without acknowledging in the slightest that there was someone else standing not six feet away.

"Excuse me," Nattie said in a hushed voice.

Callie looked up slowly. She had not been startled. "Yes," she said without removing her sunglasses.

"I know this may be a very personal question, but I have never been to a counselor before and don't know what to look for. I was just driving by and saw the sign." Nattie pointed in that direction. "Then I saw you coming out—" Hoping Callie would finish her sentence, she left it hanging.

Callie did not take the bait, and an awkward silence fell between them.

"I think I need help in dealing with my divorce from my alcoholic husband," confessed Nattie. It was mostly true. "Do you recommend this shrink? I mean, if it is not too personal."

Sliding her glasses to the top of her head, Callie made her way around the car. "She prefers the terms 'therapist' or 'counselor' to 'shrink.' Shrinks prescribe medicine," explained Callie. "And it is personal, but that is okay. I know what it feels like to need help and be afraid to ask for it." Callie stopped talking then and looked away, but not before Nattie saw the glassy expression in her eyes.

Nattie knew to keep quiet. This silence was different. Callie would return when the heaviness passed.

"I have been seeing Charlotte for close to six months. I have never been to another counselor so I cannot compare, but she has helped me." Then looking back at Nattie, she added, "I think she could help you, too."

Nattie extended her hand. "I am Natasha." This one was marginally true.

"I am Callie." She took Nattie's hand. Her grip was firm.

"Six months?" asked Nattie in an attempt to keep Callie talking.

Callie nodded.

"I don't think I could afford six months. Does it always take that long?"

"I am sure that it varies with the issue."

"And you are dealing with something that is taking six months?"

Callie looked at her and, for the first time, showed a trace of a smile. "I am."

"I am sorry," said Nattie quickly. "That was way too personal. I don't know what I was thinking."

"That is okay. In fact, Charlotte has encouraged me to open up to someone, but—" She hesitated. "—it's hard for me to trust people."

"I know we just met, but I'm here and my friends tell me I am a good listener."

Callie's smile disappeared and a look of sadness crossed her face.

"Do you want to get a cup of coffee or something?"

Callie looked at her watch. "I can't. I'm sorry, but I can't."

"That's okay. I understand," Nattie said, assuming the voice of one used to being a victim.

"Do you know the Blackbird Bakery?"

Nattie nodded.

Callie put her sunglasses back on. "Well, I have another appointment now, but I could meet you there on Monday morning for that cup of coffee if you want."

"How about Tuesday at 10 o'clock? They are closed on Mondays."

"Tuesday then," replied Callie with a nod. Then, without another word, she got into her car and drove off, leaving a confused private detective standing in the driveway.

CHAPTER 18

SATURDAY WITH DEBBIE AND DUANE

"Are you Nattie?" asked the man who answered the front door of Debbie's home.

"I am, and you must be Duane."

Duane was a man of average height, but his thinness made him look small. His dress was odd for a Saturday afternoon—a short-sleeved, green-striped, button-down shirt tucked into a pair of slacks pulled up just a bit too high. From the neck down he looked as close to Ed Grimley as anyone Nattie had ever seen. From the neck up he looked like a clean-cut frat boy with a big grin.

"I am. Good to finally meet you. Come on in," he said, holding the door open.

Nattie handed him a bottle of Merlot she had just picked up from Inari Wines. "I hope red is okay."

Duane took the bottle by the neck and looked at the label. "It's perfect, but you didn't have to do that."

"Where's Debbie?"

"Follow me."

Nattie followed him through the living room and the kitchen and out onto a deck where Debbie was grilling steaks.

"Hey Nattie. Are you feeling better?"

"I am."

Debbie poked at one of the steaks. "It is good to get past that kind of thing."

I wish I was past it.

"Look, Deb. Nattie brought us a bottle of wine."

"Well, I was going to bring a pie, but there just wasn't enough time to learn how to bake a pie."

Duane laughed a little too hard. "I'll go open this," he said.

"He's trying to make a good impression," explained Debbie. She leaned closer. "I think he is hoping you need a dentist."

They ate on the deck. The steaks were perfectly done, as were the sweet potatoes and green beans. Duane was in change of the salad and he put too on much honey mustard dressing. At least he got the bacon bits just right.

"Is this real bacon?" asked Nattie.

"No," answered Duane through a mouthful of salad.

"Actually," interjected Debbie softly, "it is real bacon."

Looking at her sternly, "I took them out of a Bacon Bits dispenser about ten minutes ago."

"I know, but after we used that up I keep refilling it with bacon bits I make."

"Are you serious?"

"I know how much you like them."

Duane's expression softened. Turning towards Nattie, "Isn't she something?"

"She is," agreed Nattie.

Patting Debbie on the hand, "She's a regular little homemaker."

Debbie winced.

"How's your steak?" he asked Nattie.

"Perfect."

"And your salad?"

"I think Nattie might have preferred to have her dressing on the side," answered Debbie. "Most women like …"

"With a wave of his hind he interrupted her, "Oh well, it saves time if I just do it. Okay with you Nattie?"

"My salad is delicious," answered Nattie reflexively.

"You see," he said to Debbie, then turning to Nattie, "she worries too much."

Debbie's head was down.

"Want to hear why we have such a great marriage?"

Not while your wife is shut down.

"Please don't," begged Debbie.

"It's just a joke," he took a large gulp of the wine. "It was on our honeymoon and we were taking one of those donkey tours to the bottom of the Grand Canyon. The donkey stopped and would not go on so I got off and told the donkey, 'that's one.' After we got going again the donkey stopped suddenly and I fell off. So I told the donkey, 'that's two.' While I was standing there the donkey hit me with his head so I took out a revolver and shot the donkey in the head. That's when Debbie here said 'what did you do that for?' So I looked at her and told her, 'that's one.'" He laughed.

Debbie mouthed, 'I'm sorry,' across the table.

Nattie smiled politely and filled her mouth with salad. It was an old joke. Nattie had heard it many times, but this was the first time that the teller was also the one with the revolver.

"We've had a great marriage ever since."

Debbie touched his forearm gently, "Duane honey, would you go back inside and get the pepper?"

"Sure," taking a bite of steak he excused himself.

Leaning across the table once Duane was inside Debbie whispered, "Please don't judge him harshly. He's nervous about making a good impression."

He should be. He's an insensitive dork. "Oh, don't worry about that. I know he's just trying too hard."

"Thanks Nattie. He's actually really sweet."

As long as he's not counting.

Emerging back outside, "I couldn't find the pepper."

"Oops," blurted Debbie, "here it is on the table. I'm sorry."

"Space Queen," announced Duane in a high pitched sing songy voice.

That's one.

CHAPTER 19

SUNDAY LUNCH AT THE O'BRIENS

The Sunday tradition at the O'Brien house was Sunday school, church, and a family midday meal, which was generally the biggest meal of the week. The meal was always followed by a conversation that Nattie and Kevin referred to, when they were young, as the "Inquisition." Inquisitions began with a shift from mealtime banter to a lower, slower tone and moved to Lionel's expressing his "concern" about something either Kevin or Nattie was doing. When he used the word "concern," however, he really meant that he disapproved.

As they grew out of adolescence and into early adulthood, the Inquisitions faded and a new form of after lunch conversation emerged. Under the guise of leading an open discussion, Lionel would ask what each member of the family thought about the sermon or, if the sermon did not meet his purpose, some other topic of his choosing. Everyone would have a time to speak his or her piece, and Lionel would listen intently. Lionel's turn to share, which always came last, was a lecture. If no one asked a question or made a comment, then they would consider themselves lucky if his turn on the soapbox was a half hour or less. The experience as a captive audience made them long for the days of the Inquisition.

It was no surprise, then, that once they moved away from the O'Brien home, their resistance of the Sunday ritual bordered on rudeness. Nattie and Kevin made a pact between themselves to make an appearance at the Sunday ritual once every three months and always together. This, they reasoned, fulfilled their duty as children and kept their resistance from being too obvious. On rare occasions, one of the two of them was cornered into accepting an invitation. When this happened, the one cornered was on his or her own. The other was free to lend support or not.

Nattie was the one cornered for this Sunday. Kevin was not obliged to attend, but here he was nonetheless. Nattie knew that of the two of them he was the more flexible and easy going. He could find a way to amuse himself no matter where he was. It was a quality in him that she often admired. It was a quality that occasionally made her want to strangle him. Today, it was working out for her.

"Can I see you for a moment?" asked Lionel ushering her from the entry to his study.

Nattie did not answer, but followed him from the foyer.

"I just wanted to commend you once again for backing off your investigation of Mrs. Trainor." His face took on that "scrunched-up" appearance, as Nattie called it, that Lionel always assumed when he was preparing to say something he was sure would be profound. "The poor woman has just lost her husband and needs all the consideration we can give her."

Who is this "we" you are referring to? If Gil Peters was paying you, then would he need all of the consideration I could give him?

"I know your job is important to you."

Well, thank you for not referring to it as my little job.

"You are so talented. I am sure there are plenty of other jobs out there for you."

Nattie smiled. There was no reason to alert him to her real thoughts. "Thank you. That is nice for you to say, and might I say your hair looks nice today."

"Really?" he asked, somewhat surprised by her compliment.

"What are you two doing?" asked Ingrid, Nattie's mother, from the doorway. "I hope you are not discussing business on the Sabbath."

Lionel grinned and raised his hands. "Guilty, but no more."

"Good," she said. "It is time for lunch."

"Roasted chicken," Lionel informed Nattie.

"From Earth Fare?" Nattie asked her mother.

"Absolutely."

"Did you get it yesterday?"

"Oh no. I picked this up on the way home from church." Ingrid led the way to the dining room. "This is when it will be most succulent."

Joining them for lunch were Samantha, Lionel's daughter from his first marriage, and her husband, Eli Gorzilanski. Samantha and Eli, along with their twelve-year-old son, Trevor, sat across from Nattie and Kevin. Eli was also a lawyer. He worked for his father-in-law and attended his father-in-law's church. His attendance would have been noteworthy if he had not attended the Sunday lunch.

The mealtime conversation was dominated by Kevin and Eli and focused mostly on some new phone that could manage your life. This gave the rest of the family something to agree upon, namely, that these two guys were "techno-dorks." Samantha cringed whenever name-calling took place in front of Trevor.

I am sure as a twelve-year-old he has never encountered name-calling, thought Nattie. *Besides, they* are *techno-dorks. Even your father agrees. And that is why you cringe but do not say anything, isn't it, Princess?*

"I am glad to hear laughter at this table," Lionel announced in a tone that marked the transition away from laughter. "It makes me think of the sermon this morning."

The sermon that day was on the attitude of joy. According to the preacher, we are expected to be joyful even when we are in a troubled time. "It's not the same as happiness," the pastor had said. This really struck a chord in Nattie's mind because she used those two words as if they meant almost the same thing. She had always supposed that joy was a more subdued form of happiness and that happiness was a more exuberant form of joy.

What the preacher said made sense. "Happiness is a feeling; it depends on circumstances. Joy is an attitude and is independent of circumstance."

The open discussion was the best captive audience time she could remember. Lionel even seemed pleased with contributions from the less religious side of the table. Lionel's ten minutes on the soapbox set an all-time record for brevity. *Am I happy about that or joyful?* wondered Nattie before praying, *Just do not let anyone ask a question.*

At that point, Eli asked Lionel, "Could a person develop or strengthen their attitude of joy?"

"When I want to strengthen a characteristic of personality, I try to emulate someone who seems to have that characteristic."

"What does emulate mean?" asked Trevor.

"Emulate means to admire or copy something," answered his mother.

"That sounds like coveting something that belongs to your neighbor," observed the boy.

Lionel chuckled at the boy's cleverness and explained, "Coveting a neighbor's wife is what is specifically mentioned in the Bible. In fact, any coveting of any woman that is not your wife is wrong. But a quality like joy or a virtue like honesty is not the same. If your neighbor has great integrity and you admire it, then you may covet that quality for yourself. You are not trying to take his integrity; you want what he has for yourself. So Eli, I think coveting joy is okay. Yes," scanning the table to include everyone in his pronouncement, "it is okay to covet joy."

At this point, Kevin leaned over to Nattie and whispered, "But you better hope Joy's husband doesn't find out."

CHAPTER 20

BLACKBIRD BAKERY

At 10 a.m. sharp Nattie parked in front of the Blackbird Bakery on the west side of Piedmont Street and found Callie Trainor already sitting at one of the tables out front. She was reading *Ellen Foster* by Kaye Gibbons.

"How is that?" asked Nattie. "I have never read it, but several people have recommended it to me."

Before answering, Callie tucked the book away in the messenger bag sitting at her feet. "It is not exactly a fun read; but it has important things to say about kids, their parents, and the system. I think the people who would choose to read it are most likely not the ones who need to read it." Standing up and gesturing towards the door, she asked, "Do you know what you want?"

The voice in her head said, *Key lime square…key lime square…key lime square*. The voice had a hypnotic opinion about what *must* be eaten at this and several other places around Bristol. Although the squares at Blackbird Bakery came in serving sizes big enough for two or three people, it was still a hard voice to resist; but with Callie and her Katharine Hepburn body standing right behind her, Nattie ordered a large coffee. There would be other times for key lime squares.

Callie then stepped up to place her order. "A chocolate peanut butter square and a small coffee please."

A week earlier, Nattie had split a chocolate peanut butter square with a young woman named Pua, who just happened to be standing behind her in line. It was good, but the voice was still partial to the key lime.

Callie Trainor, with her Grace Kelly looks and pouty personality, was in all likelihood going to pick at her dessert for three and leave two and a half servings on the table when she left. She simply looked like the kind of woman that never had to pay attention to what something cost.

The two women made their way back to the sidewalk where the tables would be in shade until after lunch.

Callie took a healthy bite off one corner of her dessert and smiled. "I love these things," she confessed before taking a sip of coffee. Then she held up another fork. "Would you like a bite?"

"No thanks," Nattie lied.

"Are you sure? It is very good and there is plenty of it here." She lay the fork down in front of Nattie. "Just in case you change your mind."

While Callie savored each bite of her square, Nattie described her divorce from her alcoholic husband. It was an easy story to keep going because it was true. She had hoped that speaking about her husband would spark a similar disclosure from Callie, but Callie just ate and listened.

Nattie avoided asking questions for fear she would frighten Callie, so when she ran out of things to say about Nathan she began talking about her father. *Just stay connected* was her strategy for the day. Even if she learned nothing but still managed another meeting, she would be satisfied.

"My birthday is July 18th, but I did not hear from him at all. Then in August he called me out of the blue and wanted to know if I had seen the Super Bowl half-time show."

"Wasn't that in January?"

"What can I say?" Nattie shrugged. "His timing was off in all kinds of ways."

"I'm sorry," Callie said.

Nattie laughed. This, too, was a true story. "He said he heard "Teenage Wasteland" on the radio, and it made him think of the Who performing it live during the halftime show. He thought it was strange to see a bunch of sixty-year-olds sing that song."

"I think it's strange not to remember your daughter's birthday." Callie actually sounded angry on Nattie's behalf. "Let me guess," she said. "He was embarrassed that he had forgotten and was calling to check to see if you were mad about it."

"That way he can slide by without apologizing."

"Or taking responsibility," added Callie.

They studied each other for a moment before Nattie remarked, "You sound like you know what you are talking about. Is that from experience or is it from therapy?"

"Both, I think. Therapy helped me name it, but I had already noticed it," Callie said with a definite air of sadness. "Being let down by your father is about as hurtful as it gets."

Nattie reached across the table and took hold of her hand.

Callie responded by squeezing Nattie's hand, but then she let go and put her hands in her lap.

Originally, Nattie felt justified in lying because Callie had resisted being interviewed when a man's reputation and freedom were at stake. She could have been hiding something important to the case. In fact, Nattie always considered the spouse of a murder victim a suspect until cleared, and this spouse had been especially evasive. But now the lie made her feel a little dirty.

Keep your head in the game, Nattie instructed herself. *Some people can turn on the emotion. Just because she can stir up emotions in you does not mean she is innocent.* Still, Callie *felt* innocent. Nattie then had to remind herself; *This is not a time to trust your feelings.* But it was not a time to ignore them either. *Open mind. Open mind.*

While Nattie played tug of war in her head, Callie drifted off in hers. "I don't know what is wrong with me," Callie said abruptly. "I have really enjoyed talking to you, but— I don't know— I just don't do well with others."

"I don't know what you mean, Callie. I have really enjoyed talking with you. You made me feel better about my father."

"Really?"

"Yeah, really. You could be a counselor. Have you ever thought of that?"

A subtle smile crossed Callie's face. "I have not thought about that sort of thing for a long time, but I used to think about being a missionary." She shifted her weight in her chair. "I guess it is time for me to start thinking about what I'm going to do with my life again."

Nattie listened carefully for some mention about the loss of her husband, but Callie grew silent and just turned towards the street. About that time, a carload of businessmen drove by. They looked like highly successful executive types; but when they caught a glimpse of Callie, they are regressed back to junior high school. The man in the back seat came close to pressing his nose against the window.

Callie looked straight at them, but seemed not notice them at all. Instead, she returned to the conversation she had broken off. "You know, I have been on four mission trips to Darfur in the past two and a half years."

"How was it?"

"I loved it there. Those folks are incredible. In spite of everything that has happened to them, they are the nicest, friendliest people in the world." Her voice was more animated than earlier. "I felt at home."

"You went with your church, I suppose?"

"Not my church. With a mission group from right here in Bristol, MRDR. Have you ever heard of them?"

"No, I haven't. That does not mean anything, though. I do not travel in those circles."

"Maybe you should, Natasha," said Callie. It was her turn to reach across the table and squeeze Nattie's hand.

Callie's sudden reaction startled Nattie. Up until that moment Callie had acted like she was allergic to touch. She had barely tolerated Nattie's attempt to hold her hand; now she was initiating it herself.

The moment did not last long before Callie looked at her watch and said, "Excuse me a moment." Then she got up and went back into the bakery.

A minute later she returned with a small Styrofoam take-home box. She put the remains of her chocolate peanut butter square—slightly more than half a square—into the box and handed it to Nattie. "Chocolate is a horrible thing to waste."

Is that a joke? "I agree, but I can't take it. It's yours."

"I want you to," she said. "Besides, there's already a half of one of these in my fridge at home." Then she hooked her bag over her shoulder. "I'm on my way to see Charlotte now, and I have another appointment next Tuesday at 11. If you want to, we could meet here again next week?"

"Only if you let me get us the square to split. I want you to try my favorite, Key Lime."

Callie just smiled and walked towards the library where her Honda was parked.

Nattie took her coffee cup in to get a refill for the road. She passed a young woman she recognized from the week before when she split a square with Pua, the youth worker from First Presbyterian Church. Nattie caught her attention as she came down the stairs from the balcony where the youth pastors gathered every Tuesday morning. "Excuse me. You are with the Youth Ministry group, aren't you?"

"I am," the young woman answered. "Paige Morgan from First Methodist. Can I help you with something?"

"I wanted some information about a group called MDRR. Have you heard of them?"

Paige's eyes twinkled when she smiled. "Sure, but it's MRDR. What do you want to know?"

"I'm just looking for general information about where they go, what they do, and who goes with them."

"I am sure they have a website. You could try that. Damian Saunders is the man you want to talk to. Are you interested in going to Darfur?"

"I'm just interested at this point, but maybe."

"Well, I know a few people who have gone with them, and they all had good experiences." Paige handed Nattie a business card. "If the web does not work, give me a call and I am sure I can get you in touch with them."

CHAPTER 21

DAMIAN SAUNDERS

Damian Saunders, the founder and director of MRDR, looked at his lunch and asked, "What was so special about this sandwich?" He had agreed to meet Nattie at Manna Bagel for lunch as he was heading there anyway.

Nattie went first and ordered the tomato basil soup instead of the soup and sandwich combination that the "voice" told her to order. She was still feeling stuffed from the half of Callie's chocolate peanut butter square she was eating while she introduced herself to Damian over the phone forty-five minutes ago.

While Nattie stood close by, Susan, the manager, suggested that he order a Natasha. She explained that it was like the grilled cheese and tomato bagel, but with onion and on a pepperoni bagel. "You will get a kick out of it," she told him, winking at Nattie.

Responding to his question Nattie handed Damian one of her business cards. "Maybe this will explain."

"Okay," he said skeptically as he took the card. "Natasha McMorales," he read aloud. "So Nattie stands for Natasha, and that is the same as the sandwich. Very cool. They named a sandwich after you."

"Nattie stands for Natalie," she explained. "Natasha is my professional name. My brother set that up while I was in Nashville and I have been explaining it ever since." She pointed over her shoulder towards the counter. "He altered their Continental Bagel sandwich and named it after me as a joke. It's not on the menu, but Susan knows what it is. So does Matthew."

Damian took a healthy bite of his sandwich and nodded his approval. "They should put this on their menu," he said. "It is very good."

"What does MRDR stand for?"

"Medical Relief for Darfur Region."

"If you don't mind me saying so, my first thought was that it was an abbreviation for the word 'murder.'"

Damian smiled, "That seems appropriate, don't you think?"

Nattie avoided answering by taking a bite of her Natasha.

"In a way, we are responding to murder; but that is still not the image we want to use so as to motivate people. Some folks look at those initials and think Mister Doctor, which isn't a bad association, either."

Nattie nodded.

As they ate Damian shared about the vision of MRDR to provide medical relief to Darfur. Teams providing various kinds of health care accompanied by non-medical volunteers were sent to various relief camps around the Darfur region of western Sudan. "We have plans for six trips to Darfur this year. This is what you wanted to talk to me about, right?"

"Partially," corrected Nattie. "I am doing a background check on someone who reports having been on one of your trips to Darfur."

"Really? Who?"

"Well Mr. Saunders—"

"Please, it is Damian."

She nodded and continued, "The person I am interested in is Callie Trainor. I cannot tell you much about the investigation. It is of a sensitive nature. But all I need is some background information. So, do you know Ms. Trainor, Damian?"

"Sure I know Callie. At least I have been on several trips to Darfur with her."

"What can you tell me about her?"

Damian lowered his eyes for a moment. Then, looking back up at Nattie, he said, "I think the best adjective is 'dignified.'"

Before Nattie could respond he added, "Yes dignified. When I first met her, I would have said she was aloof."

I have heard that description before.

"I got everyone going on that trip together several times before we left," he remembered. "I showed them pictures of where we were headed and told them what to expect. I had hoped that those gatherings would also be team- building times, but that did not click for Callie. She never shared anything very personal; and when it was time to mingle, she would just sit patiently waiting for a meeting to start. Then she would leave as soon as it was over."

"Shy?"

"I thought that too before we got to Darfur the first time," agreed Damian. "But when you speak to her, she makes very good eye contact; and when she speaks to you, she speaks with confidence. So I do not think shy really captures it either. It is more like she is not interested."

"Do you mean like conceited?"

"No, I mean like serious. Like she is not interested in superficialities."

Nattie was sure she was missing some distinction he was trying to make. It still sounded like he was describing a *prima donna.*

"You would have had to see her at the orphanage or at the hospitals. That was where she shone." He smiled as he remembered. "We were visiting a rural hospital one day and most of the team was gathered in a ward for children. But there was another ward for the terminally ill further down the hall. They told us to stay away from that room. There is still a lot of AIDS in the region, but it is getting much better," he explained.

"When I did not see Callie with the children, I went to look for her and found her in the terminal ward. She was standing next to a decrepit old man in a makeshift wheel chair. He was holding her hand and she let him nuzzle it against his cheek." Damian leaned forward against the edge of the table. "I tell you the truth, there were two nurses watching her, and I heard one of them say, 'I've never seen him do that before.' No, Nattie, Callie is not aloof or shy or conceited. Whatever it is that fuels her reservations about relating to the rest of us does not get in the way of her compassion."

"Do you think she has a psychological problem relating to others?"

"I do not know about that. Maybe she does. But if she does have a psychological problem and it makes her as compassionate as she is, then I hope God gives it to more people."

He noticed Nattie flinch. "Do I sound irreverent to you?"

"Not at all," Nattie said, "but I am pretty sure you would sound irreverent to my step father."

"I get that a lot," he shared with an expression on his face that was somewhere between pride and boyish defiance. "Do you mind if I ask you a personal question Nattie?"

"No, go ahead."

"Where are you in your faith journey?"

Nattie could feel herself tense up. She had heard that sort of question before, and it was generally followed by a lecture that left her feeling inferior and judged. "I am not sure that I believe the same things as you do. I believe there is a God and I believe He loves us. But I do not believe everything I hear at church."

"Good," he said.

"Good?" His response was completely unexpected. "Aren't you going to tell me about what you believe?"

"I would be happy to answer any question you want to ask me about what I believe; but I think as long as you are seeking answers yourself, you do not need them from me. Besides, I suspect that you have already heard too many people share what their answers are with you."

"But isn't that what evangelism is? Isn't that why you go on mission trips, to share what you believe?"

Pointing at the small wooden cross Nattie was wearing on a string around her neck, Damian asked, "Do you know what that is?"

Nattie held the "T" shaped cross with her fingertips. "It is a Franciscan cross." Then, with a measure of embarrassment, she confessed, "I kind of like Saint Francis."

"Me too," Damian agreed. "Do you know what Saint Francis said about evangelism?"

"No."

"He said, 'Evangelize wherever you go and if absolutely necessary use words.'"

CHAPTER 22

KEVIN FINISHES THE BACKGROUND CHECK

"Okay, Uncle Floyd. I will be sure to tell her," Kevin said into his phone as Nattie entered the waiting room of the Natasha McMorales Detective Agency.

"Was that Harry on the phone?" Nattie asked.

Uncle Floyd was their father's chain-smoking older brother from Galena, Illinois. When they were younger, before their father left them, the family would spend a week every summer in northern Illinois. That always meant a Cubs game at Wrigley Field with their grandfather and fishing the Mississippi River with Uncle Floyd.

One year, when Kevin was eight, Uncle Floyd surprised them all by renting a houseboat that was large enough for both families plus the grandfather. While Nattie, Ingrid, and Aunt Barbara spent the day making casseroles and cookies for the trip, all the men went to prep the boat. Kevin was given the job of draining the fuel-oil from a small pump in the hull. Uncle Floyd had added the fuel oil before he realized that it needed regular gasoline instead of fuel-oil. Kevin drained the petroleum into a paper cup, but he did not want to throw it in the river so he put it in the toilet instead. Unfortunately, Uncle Floyd sat on that toilet a few minutes later; and when he dropped his cigarette between his legs, a small explosion flashed underneath him. The flame was there and gone, taking every hair it came in contact with, before Floyd knew what had happened. That was the day he became "Harry."

"Yeah, that was Harry," answered Kevin.

She waited for more, but it did not come. "Well? What did you tell him that you going to tell me?"

Kevin knit his eyebrow and cocked his head. Then the light bulb came on. "Ah," he said, "you heard me tell him that."

"I did. What is it about?"

"Nothing. He calls once a week and says he wants to hire you to find something for him."

Nattie just stared at him.

Kevin rolled his hands over, trying to coax her to awareness. "You know— He wants you to find something he lost—on that houseboat."

Nattie rolled her eyes, sighed, and headed for her office.

"How was your morning?" he asked, following her from his desk. "With Ms Trainor?"

Nattie thought about it before answering, "I really do not know." She remembered what Beau, the bartender from Barley Corners, had said, "She is either completely innocent or she is one cold-hearted liar." Nattie looked up from her desk. "And I have no idea which."

"Well, I may be able to make it even more confusing for you."

I would be surprised if you couldn't.

"I have been doing a background check on her like you asked."

She sat up straighter. "Did you find out something good?"

"Not exactly."

"Okay, Kevin, I give up. What did you find out?"

"Nothing— nothing at all."

She smirked. "Well, that was worth waiting for."

"You don't understand. There is nothing to find. No birth record, no credit record, no school records." He leaned on the desk. "Your Callie Trainor does not exist."

CHAPTER 23

TO DC

Kevin's internet search did uncover a document verifying Callie's marriage to Norris Trainor. According to her marriage license her maiden name was Samms. The Samms name did not produce any new possibilities in the search for her identity. Before she got married, Callie had worked at National University Law School in Washington, DC. Kevin knew this because there was a record of one payroll check issued to a Callie Trainor one week after her wedding date. Presumably this was her severance check, which meant that either she only worked for one week or she might have been working there under another name before she got married. A quick call to the payroll department at National hit a blockade when Nattie was told that she would have to fill out a "Request for Records" form in person.

What did I expect from a law school? wondered Nattie.

Before heading off, Nattie called London to get an okay on continuing the investigation and the extra expenses a trip to DC would entail. It was more of a courtesy call than a request for permission since their initial contract had given her permission enough to do whatever was necessary on Gil Peters' behalf. She knew London would okay any expense. Still, it was also just a good business practice to keep the customer in the loop. She got the thumbs up she expected.

So as to miss the DC traffic, she left at 6:00 in the morning. If all went perfectly, she could be there by 2:00 in the afternoon and on her way home by 3:00, well before the commuters left the city. It surprised her to find a parking place on the street in front of the building.

Could this be an omen? she wondered as she locked her car. *Could I really be on my way out of the city by 3:30?* The answer would come quickly.

National University Law School occupied the third, fourth, and fifth floors of an office building on Third Street, five blocks from the Mall. The executive offices were on the third floor, faculty offices and classrooms on the fourth, and the library on the fifth. Nattie went to the third floor and found a door marked "PAYROLL." Just inside the door of the office, she found a chest-high counter beyond which was an open area containing a half dozen desks and a row of file cabinets against the back wall. Three of the desks were occupied, all by women. A fourth woman stood behind the counter.

"Is there a Brenda Osterhaus?" Nattie asked.

"I'm Brenda Osterhaus," answered one of the women, looking up from the computer keyboard where she was working. "Can I help you?"

Nattie introduced herself. "I am Nattie Moreland. I talked to you yesterday about getting copies of employment records for a Callie Samms. I believe I need to fill out some forms."

"Oh yes, I remember," said Brenda. "Just wait one moment. I will be right back."

Brenda went to a closed door to Nattie's left and after opening it leaned in and said something Nattie could not hear. A moment later another woman walked past her and came to the counter.

"I am Francis Oberman, the Human Resources Director here at National University. I understand you are interested in one of our former employees."

"Yes," answered Nattie, getting nervous at the unexpected shift in formality. "I drove here from Bristol, Tennessee, this morning because I was told that I would need to fill out a Request Form in person. Is there a problem?"

"Could I see some identification please?"

"Certainly." Nattie handed the woman a business card and opened her wallet to display her PI license.

Francis studied the license and then the card before continuing, "Can I ask what this is about, Ms Moreland?"

Nattie could feel the muscles tighten across her shoulders. This was the first time she had given out her business card without being asked to explain that she was not actually named Natasha McMorales. It was a sign, she reasoned, of how seriously Francis Oberman was taking their conversation.

Nattie decided to tell the truth, *mostly*. "Mrs. Trainor, formerly Ms Samms, is a key witness in a case that I am not at liberty to reveal. In cases like the one I am involved with, it is simply normal to do background checks on the key witnesses."

"I see," said Francis with a frown.

With mounting frustration Nattie decided to push. "Look, Ms Oberman, I came here in good faith. I called first, I was told what I needed to do, and I have done it. Had I needed a court order I would have—"

Francis quickly interrupted her, "There is no need for that. We would be delighted to help you with your investigation," pausing she glanced at Brenda Osterhaus, "if we could—"

"If?" It was Nattie's turn to interrupt.

Francis' demeanor had shifted from parental disbelief to adolescent backtracking. What you were told when you spoke with Mrs. Osterhaus yesterday on the phone was, as you say, in good faith. We do have Request for Information forms, and that is normally all that would be required. This situation, however, is different."

"How is it different?"

Looking extremely embarrassed, Francis lowered her eyes. "I do not know how to say this any other way, but—we do not seem to have that file."

CHAPTER 24

NATIONAL UNIVERSITY

"I'm sorry?" Nattie said on reflex. A missing personnel file was quite a coincidence. She had become skeptical of coincidences.

Brenda stepped forward from where she had been standing slightly behind her supervisor, "After I spoke to you I went to pull that file, but I could not find it." She looked sheepishly at Francis. "We combed through those files yesterday, but it is not here."

Francis quickly added, "This has never happened before."

Nattie leaned against the front of the counter. "Maybe you could tell me what you remember about Callie Samms, then."

Brenda and Francis looked at each other before Francis answered, "We did not know her. In this department we usually keep to ourselves."

"We know what everyone makes," Brenda began.

"And who has what medical insurance claims. It separates us from the rest of the employees," Francis explained.

"We like it that way, though," offered Brenda.

The conversation had taken a completely unhelpful turn, so Nattie tried another tack. "If neither of you knew Ms Samms personally, could you at least direct me to someone who did?"

"She worked for President Allen," answered Brenda. Francis frowned.

President Thomas Allen's office was at the other end of the third floor, but his assistant said he was at a meeting and would not be back until the next day. Nattie tried to make an appointment, but was told that his next opening was not until the following week. Explaining that it was an urgent matter concerning Callie Samms, Nattie left her cell phone number.

"He will call for his messages," his assistant claimed. "I cannot, of course, guarantee that he will have time to call back."

"That is okay," Nattie tried to sound appreciative of the assistant's efforts, "but please tell him that is my cell phone and he is welcome to call me any time day or night."

It was 3 o'clock when Nattie exited the building. Her question was answered. She would not be headed home by 3:30 unless the Residence Inn Hotel across the street could be considered home. Luckily, there was a vacancy. She was checked into her room and on her way to the Smithsonian Air and Space Museum before it closed at 5:00.

Once in the museum, she just wandered until she found herself standing at the Wright Brothers exhibit. She wondered if the plane she could almost touch was the same one flown at Kitty Hawk and had begun to search for the identifying plaque when her vibrating cell phone drove curiosity from her mind.

"Hello."

"Hello, is this Ms. Morales?" It was a man's voice.

"This is Nattie Moreland of the Natasha McMorales Detective Agency. How can I help you?"

"This is Thomas Allen. I believe you came by to see me this afternoon."

"Yes I did. Thank you for getting back to me. I wonder if I could set up a meeting with you."

"To discuss Callie?"

"Yes sir."

"Is Callie okay?"

"I do not know her myself," Nattie said. "I am just doing a background check on her. I understand that she was your assistant for a while. Is that correct?"

102

"Yes it is. She worked for me for a little over a year, but other than Christmas letters I have not had any contact with her for the last three or four years."

"I understand that, sir. And I understand that you are a very busy man. I would, however, appreciate any time you could give me. It would help me immensely."

"Well," he said slowly. "I will be at a luncheon meeting with the Smithsonian Board tomorrow until 1 o'clock, and I have to meet with some Trustees at 2:30; but I could meet you after 1 if you would be willing to meet me at a museum cafeteria."

"Oh absolutely. Thank you. Which museum?"

"The National Museum of the American Indian. Do you know where it is?"

"No," Nattie answered, "but I am at the Air and Space Museum right now and I can ask at the information desk."

"Well, the American Indian Museum is right next door. And now, if you will excuse me I will say good afternoon."

"Where exactly are we meeting?"

"When you come in the front door, you will see a large spiral stairway across the lobby. You cannot miss it. Why don't we meet at the bottom of that stairway?"

"Great. And thank you again for meeting me."

"No problem. By the way, I'm kind of tall and skinny with thinning red hair and glasses."

"And I look a little like I could be Kristen Bell's sister." Nattie was always embarrassed to compare herself to the beautiful Veronica Mars actress, but it was what most folks told her about her looks and was the simplest way of describing herself.

The elderly man at the information desk of the Air and Space Museum told Nattie, "If you like seafood I would recommend the Legal Seafood restaurant. Their clam chowder has been served at every Presidential inaugural since the mid 1980's.

Nattie bought a day-pass for the Metro at the Federal Center SW station and then took the blue line to L'Enfant Plaza, transferred to the green line, and got out in Chinatown. From there it was a two-block walk to Legal Seafood on 7th Street. She ordered a house salad and the crab cakes from the appetizer menu.

The clam chowder may be famous, but it is still clam chowder, she reasoned behind slightly clinched teeth, her normal reaction to clams.

The crab cakes were the absolute best she had ever eaten. She followed dinner with a Warm Chocolate Pudding Cake served with vanilla ice cream, chocolate sauce, and a coconut cookie. An espresso topped the meal off perfectly.

By 8:30 that evening she was back at the Residence Inn soaking in a warm bath and reading the last three chapters of *Murder Takes the Cake* by Gayle Trent.

CHAPTER 25

THE LINCOLN MEMORIAL

The complementary breakfast at the hotel was excellent. Nattie had a toasted bagel, scrambled eggs, sausage, and an assortment of melon cubes. She was checked out by 9:00 and decided to spend the morning strolling from one end of the Mall to the other.

Starting on the lawn in front of the Capitol Building, she headed toward the Lincoln Memorial. She passed by the Washington Monument, but did not stop. She had been to the monument during a high school trip and had even taken the elevator ride to the top. It was not a pleasant memory. At the top, the park ranger had explained that the monument was made of cut stones, but had no mortar. Being that high up in the air was bad enough, but the thought of standing on a loose pile of stones sent a chill up her spine.

The semi-leisurely walk from the Capitol put her at the foot of the Lincoln Memorial before 10 o'clock. Nattie's previous trips to DC always included seeing something of historical importance, but never this one. And this one was the one she most wanted to see.

Climbing the massive stairs in front, she arrived at the top more out of breath than she expected. Or maybe finally standing in front of the statue took her breath away. She had heard that there was a spot for making eye contact with Lincoln. It was crowded with people taking turns photographing one another. Nattie maneuvered through the crowd to take her turn looking up into Lincoln's face. It was true. He did appear to be looking back.

"Would you mind?" someone asked, touching her arm.

Nattie's eyes fell upon a twenty-something man in a black tee shirt holding out a camera.

He gestured towards a young woman in front of the statue. "Would you take a Picture of us?"

Nattie took a photograph of them standing where everyone else stood for Pictures and then she asked, "How about coming forward and taking one with his face between your faces?"

They allowed her to pose them; and when she was finished taking the Pictures, these were their favorite shots. Only after receiving their lavish praise did she notice what was written on the black tee shirt.

> *I am a firm believer in the people. If given the truth, they can be depended upon to meet any national crisis. The great point is to bring them the real facts, and beer.*
>
> *A. Lincoln*

"Is that really an authentic Abe Lincoln quote?" Nattie asked skeptically.

"I guess so." The young man turned both his palms up in an "I don't have a clue" gesture.

"It came from Ford's Theatre, though." The girl slid her arm around her companion's waist and steered him away from Nattie.

"Thanks again," he called over his shoulder.

The view across the Reflecting Pool captured the full reflection of the Washington Monument beyond. Taking some pictures of the monument with her phone brought her to the edge of the stair where she teetered ever so slightly. She had not really lost her balance, but here she was again catching her breath as she looked at that *mortar less stack of stones.*

As steep as the stairs looked from the bottom, they were even more daunting from the top. She moved to her right and descended them so that she could catch herself on the wall if need be. Near the bottom, where a fall was probably not fatal, she sat on the wall for a moment to catch her breath.

From this perch she discovered an unexpected feature of the steep stairway. From just a few steps behind, a visitor would find himself in the position of looking up sharply at the person ahead of him. Not quite straight up. But if the woman's dress was on the short side, then it was close enough. Nattie also observed that short skirts were much more the norm in DC than in Bristol.

What a goldmine for junior high boys. Just then, she noticed two real live junior high boys who seemed to have made the same discovery as she had. They followed a woman up the stairs; but when they got near the top they stopped, punched each other in the arm, and returned to the bottom to wait for their next viewing.

Nattie approached them. "Excuse me, boys. My name is Natasha McMorales, and I am on assignment for the Travel Channel doing a feature on the monuments of DC. I was wondering if I could get a few quotes from you." Both boys stopped snickering. The taller, slimmer boy immediately took a half-step back; but the shorter, more athletic one squared his shoulders and looked Nattie in the eyes. "Sure thing," he said. "What do you want to know?"

Nattie took a notepad and pen from her bag. "Well, first I want to make sure I spell your names accurately, so if you do not mind— What are your names?"

The boy nearest her looked back at his friend, who stepped forward and answered, "I am Eric Holder. They call me Eri."

After getting Eri's phone number and address, Nattie turned to the one she deemed the leader. "And you?"

"I am Mark Andrews, and they call me Mark." After giving a phone number and address, he added, "So what's you question?"

"Well boys," she said, as she put the notebook and pen away, "I was just wondering what your mothers would think if I sent them the film I just took of your peeping-Tom routine on the stairs?"

With that, the taller boy turned and ran away.

"I guess he did not like the sound of that," observed Nattie.

Mark nodded. "I don't guess he did." Backing slowly away, he began grinning. "But that's because he gave you his real name." Mark, or whoever he was, tilted his head back and laughed hard as he strolled away in the same direction his friend had run.

There goes a future senator, thought Nattie.

CHAPTER 26

THOMAS ALLEN

With an hour-and-a-half to kill before she met Mr. Allen, Nattie had plenty of time for lunch. The walk back up the Mall was enough to build up a hunger. The cafeteria at the American Indian Museum was an unexpected treasure. Most museum food was generic—salads with wilted lettuce or sandwiches on stale bread. But the American Indian Museum cafeteria was different.

Nattie spent fifteen minutes walking from station to station before settling on Buffalo Chili over fried flat bread. On the side she had a watermelon and green tomato salad and something that tasted like spiced potatoes. The food was not only unusual, but delicious as well.

"You look like Kristen Bell's twin to me, Ms Moreland," came a voice from the stairway above where Nattie waited.

Nattie had been watching the front entrance, but turned towards the voice. "Mr. Allen?"

"At your service," he said as he came to stand near her. He did not do what tall folks often did—stand so close as to force her to look up at him. He motioned towards the cafeteria. "Can I buy you lunch? They have great food here."

"I just ate in there. Thank you. It was great."

"Something to drink then?" he suggested.

Thomas Allen recommended the hot chocolate. "It is Mexican hot chocolate, so it is much creamier than what we Americans usually get."

With their respective cups of cocoa in hand they found a table in the corner. As expected, he asked for her credentials and for the purpose of the investigation. She gave her usual explanation of the Natasha McMorales name. Then she told him that although her interest in Callie Trainor was primarily background as to her credibility as a witness, it had become more involved when they were unable to find a paper trial of her history.

"How can I help you?" he asked when she was done.

"For starters, why don't you just tell me what you know about Callie?" It was Nattie's standard interview technique—to let others share what they thought was important before she asked any questions. When you did not know what the interviewee knew, then questions could just as easily take you away from important information as it could lead you to it.

"Callie worked for me for a year or a little more. I had just been hired to be the president at National. My predecessor was offered a job at the Pentagon and he took his executive assistant with him. I soon realized that my executive assistant would have to be hired from outside the university."

"Why was that?"

Thomas shook his head. "It was a mess, an absolute mess. The former president had isolated himself from most of the faculty and staff and surrounded himself with a cabinet that was more concerned with protecting and expanding their own spheres of influence than serving the needs of the institution. I knew I could not hire someone from within that hornet's nest. It would have thrown off the balance of power in ways I could not have guessed."

"Why Callie?"

Thomas looked up and off to the left as if searching for his next words. "She was not intimidated by me or impressed by my position and she had a way of telling me the truth."

"Those are sure interesting qualities for getting her a job as your assistant," observed Nattie.

"Maybe," he agreed, "but not unprecedented. Lincoln composed his cabinet almost entirely of his political rivals."

"Why did he do that?"

"I suppose he just wanted the best. Apparently he did not consider the trait of agreeing with him as a much of a criterion for the job."

"I would assume it took some confidence or courage to do that."

"Probably both," Allen replied. "But hiring Callie did not take either for me."

"So the qualification you relied on to hire Callie was that she was not intimidated or impressed."

"And she told me the truth," he repeated. "At least she made me made me consider what was right."

"Did she develop this skill while working at another college?" asked Nattie, hoping to get information about what Callie did prior to working for him.

"No. She worked the morning shift at a little coffee shop up near Georgetown University. It was before my wife moved here, and I had breakfast there nearly every morning. It was far enough away from National so that I would not run into someone who wanted something from me. Besides, the coffee was good."

"You hired the coffee girl with no higher education experience instead of a seasoned executive assistant."

"I did."

"She is very attractive," Nattie observed before she could catch herself.

"She is," agreed Thomas. "And I think she may know it, but I do not think she places any importance in her beauty one way or another." Then leaning forward, he added, "In fact, after you get to know her, which is a trick in itself, you do not notice her attractiveness anymore."

"You say she is hard to get to know."

He nodded his head. "She is not shy, nor is she without confidence; but she is the most non-assertive person I know. Not that she's a pushover, mind you. Several high-ranking folks at National tried to sidestep her to get to me, but quickly discovered how immovable she could be if she were pushed. But I digress. Yes, Ms. Moreland, she is hard to get to know."

"Did you get to know her?"

"I think I did. I do not know anything about her childhood or her family, but I know her character and I will be a character witness for her if need be. Integrity, honesty, and stability—that is who she is. And you can quote me on that."

His reference to being a character witness for Callie made Nattie wonder if he knew she was also a suspect. "Did you know all that when you hired her from the coffee shop?"

He seemed to consider the question before he answered. "Yes. I think I had an inkling anyway. Would you like to hear about the conversations we would have at the coffee shop?"

"I would."

He leaned back. "It was the early days of a new job. I went home nearly every night angry or frustrated about something—a procedure that did nothing except protect the turf of some perfunctory, or a squabble over who should do what and who should get what. Every morning, I would vent to Callie. I did not tell her too much at first, but she was so easy to talk to that it was not long before I considered her my most important confidant."

"Integrity, honesty, stability, and a good listener," repeated Nattie. "Did she give you good advice?"

Thomas laughed. "Advice? No. She never gave me any advice at all. When I had finished complaining about each new problem, she would simply ask me one question: what's the right thing to do? Can you imagine that? Reminding me to do the right thing was her gift to me. It was invaluable."

Nattie knew she was running out of time. What she really wanted to know was whether Callie Trainor could have used all those wonderful qualities to get away with murdering her husband. Instead, she asked, "You've said you did not know anything about Callie's childhood, but do you have any impressions about her family or where she grew up?"

Thomas' eyebrows went up, as if something just dawned on him. "I remember going to speak at the University of North Carolina in Asheville once, and she told me about a restaurant there that she really loved. I think it was called Salsa's. It sounded like she was pretty familiar with the city."

"Asheville?"

"Yes," he said waving his finger, "in fact it was a little before Thanksgiving and she said I had to go to The Grove Park Inn to see the gingerbread house contest. I'm positive she was from there, but I'm sure you can get more accurate information from the payroll department. I will call Francis Oberman. She is the director of human resources. She can get you anything you need." He noticed Nattie's reaction. "I am sorry. Is something wrong?"

Seeing no way around telling the president of the school that the personnel records of his institution were not as secure as they should be, Nattie grit her teeth and began. "I was there yesterday. You are right; they were quite willing to be helpful—" She hesitated.

"But?"

"But Callie Trainor's personnel file is missing."

Scowling, Thomas Allen glanced away. When he turned back, he still looked very serious, "I am not sure if this is a coincidence, Ms Moreland; but shortly after Callie left, something from my office came up missing as well."

"What was it, sir?"

Locking his eyes with hers, he replied, "My address book."

CHAPTER 27

BREAKFAST WITH DEBBIE

Kevin did not make the Monday morning breakfast at the Sunny Side Up Grill, but Debbie did. Nattie had her usual. Debbie was on her cell phone and had been since she entered the restaurant. She mouthed "same thing" to the waitress as she pointed back and forth between Nattie and herself.

"Look Duane." She finally got a word in. Up until then she had only listened. "I did tell you I would be gone this morning." Another long pause passed while she just listened again. "No, Duane, there's no one here except Nattie and me." She looked at Nattie and rolled her eyes. "Yes, anything else?" Another wait. Finally, Debbie looked at her phone and then hung up without saying good-bye.

"He's a little stressed. The dentist he is working for does not let him do as much as he said he would before we moved."

"That's tough."

"It really is. He's a good dentist. It just takes time to build a practice."

"I'm sure."

The waitress brought their coffees.

"Are you okay?" asked Nattie.

"Me?" Debbie looked surprised to be asked this question. "I'm just worried about Duane. He is under so much pressure. School loans are coming due, and he wants to do well for his dad."

"He's not—a jealous kind of guy, is he?"

"Jealous? What made you ask that?"

"I don't know. It just sounded like he was giving you the third degree about whoever else was here with you."

"No, he's just kidding about that."

Their breakfast came, just in time.

As soon as she was finished with her meal, Debbie scooted her chair back and wiped her mouth. Looking towards the door to the kitchen, "Sorry to eat and run; I have a bunch of errands to run."

Nattie, still savoring her coffee, waved her hand. "Go on, I'll get the check."

"Oh thank you Nattie. I'll get the next one," Debbie promised as she hurried out.

Nattie watched her hunch over her cell phone as soon as she was outside.

CHAPTER 28

KEVIN'S DISCOVERY

Nattie pushed the replay button on the answering machine. "Nattie, this is Alan Poe [pause] from Johnson City [pause] from high school. I was wondering if maybe, if you wanted to, that is, have dinner together sometime. There's a great pizza place called Scratch that opened since we graduated. They make everything from scratch; bread, dough, sausage. They even smoke their own meats in a wood burning brick oven. The smells in there are addictive. If you haven't tried it yet, I would love to take you there sometime. Anyway [pause] it was great to see you again the other day. Give me a call if you want. Bye."

She stared at the phone, trying to decide if his lack of sophistication in asking for a date was a positive thing or a negative thing.

"How was your trip to Washington?" asked Kevin from the doorway to the office.

Hitting the erase button, she said, "Not as productive as I had hoped."

He circled her as she stood at his desk where the answering machine was kept. He had a devilish grin on his face, but that was not unusual. He usually had a devilish grin on his face. It did mean that he was about to say something that amused him. "Wow, an unproductive trip. Does that mean you did not find a good place to eat?"

She punched him in the arm. "You know better than that. I found the best place for crab cakes and the best place for Indian food."

"Better than Sahib's?" he asked as he rubbed his arm.

"Not India Indians. Native American Indians."

"You know," Kevin said, straightening up with excitement, "you could write a book about your favorite places to eat. You might as well turn your obsession with food into something profitable."

"Is Pendant Ink looking for a food book?"

Pendant Ink was one of the thousands of money-making ideas that passed through Kevin's brain. He wanted to name his publishing company Pendant Ink because Elaine Benis from the *Seinfeld* TV show worked at Pendant Publishing. He was still promising Ollie Ruggiliano to publish a book of his recipes, "as soon as enough recipes are collected." His own book, *A Beginners Guide to Italy*, was nothing more than a title and three unedited chapters.

"You make fun of it, big sister, but it does not have to be a national bestseller for it to be profitable. If you filled it with local places, you can market it locally." He put his backpack on the desk. "Every place that you give a good shout-out to is going to want a copy and would be willing to sell them for you on commission."

"I will get back to you on that," she said. "But right now, this case I am on is about to drive me crazy."

He sat down at his desk. "Tell me about it. I am all yours."

Is that a curse? she wondered.

Sitting on the edge of the desk, she said, "I went to National and talked to the payroll department. No one there knew anything except that Callie's personnel file was missing."

"Her file was missing?"

Nattie nodded.

"That is curious."

"I also talked to the president of the school. That is who she worked for," explained Nattie. "He absolutely adores her, but does not know anything about her before he hired her."

"He adores her?"

"Yes. It is the strangest thing. Everyone who knows her at a distance thinks she is aloof and cold, but everyone who knows her more personally raves about her."

"You spent time with her," Kevin reminded his sister. "What was your impression?"

"I think she looks like Grace Kelly, and she acts like Audrey Hepburn."

"There is nothing adorable about those two," he sarcastically observed. "Is that your gut opinion?"

Nattie sighed. She was caught up short by the question. "Yes and no."

Kevin flipped he hand. "Well, that clears it up."

Nattie recalled the words of Beau the bartender again and continued. "I think she is either the most wonderful person I have ever met or she is one cold-hearted sociopath. And I go back and forth about which one it is. On one hand, there is the award-winning personality that put doing what is right above all else. On the other, there is her resistance to being interviewed and the complete absence of a past."

"And there's the missing file. Who do you think took it?"

"If I had to guess, I would say she did. Theft does not make her guilty of murder, but it fits with how hard she is working to cover up her past."

"Do you mean she might be making sure no one from her past, like a guy she went to high school with, tracks her down?"

Nattie stuck out her jaw towards her brother and tried to look menacing.

Kevin did not let up. "She probably wants to make sure no one asks her out for pizza." He ran his finger over the top of the answering machine.

"Okay, Kevin, when did that message come in?"

He looked up at her innocently and spoke in his most childlike voice. "Do you mean that message you erased when I walked in? The one from Edgar Alan Poe's great grandson?"

Hopping off the desk, she bent over him and threatened, "How would you like me to call mom and tell her it was you who dyed Lionel's cat blue?"

Putting his palms up in mock surrender, "It came on Thursday while you were in Washington. But do not worry. I called him back and told him you were out of town on a case."

"And—" she said, still bending over him.

"And he asked when you would be back."

"Aaaand!"

"And I told him you could be back in a day or it could be a couple of weeks."

She stood up and took a step back.

"Did I do good?"

"Yeah, you did, thanks."

"And Sis."

"Yes?"

"The next time you threaten me, do so with something that I'll believe you would actually do."

She tipped her head as if to say, "oh well," and asked, "Was it too strong?"

"Yes. But I'll give you this—the glare with your eyes was better. Have you been practicing?"

She punched him in the arm again and went into her office.

Kevin followed her and sat in one of the two chairs in front of her desk. "So, Sis, are you going to give Mr. Poe the time of day?"

She sat down in her own chair and picked up her mail. As if it were rehearsed a hundred times they each leaned back and put their feet up on her desk at the same time. Placing the mail in her lap, she answered, "I don't know. I am divorced so I am a free agent. But I am not sure I am ready. If I *was* ready, I could do a lot worse than him." Shaking her head, "I don't know."

Kevin knew she was not done, so he sat patiently and watched her.

"Then again, Nathan seems to be ready. He has been dating someone for a while."

"Randi Lester."

"I'm sorry?"

"The woman he is dating," he explained. "Her name is Randi Lester."

Nattie took her feet down. "Okay, Kevin, let's have it. What else do you know?"

"I know she is 33 with the body of an 18-year-old centerfold model."

"How would you like me to hold you under water for a while?" she asked, borrowing a Kevin Costner line from *Open Range*.

He spread his hands apart. "You see. There you go again making a threat you would never do."

"Get out!"

119

"But there is more. Besides the body of a centerfold model, do you know what else she has?"

"Do I look like I want to play twenty questions about this?"

Kevin held up his index finger, "She has a husband."

Nattie froze and looked at him without speaking.

"What do you think about holding her head under water for a while?"

Nattie snarled. "Are you sure about this?"

"Absolutely. I was at Our House with Ox Singleton, and she came in to see Nathan. Ox played the guitar at her wedding six years ago. He recognized her. It took me fifteen minutes on the computer to verify it. She is definitely married. Her husband is a Pilot—pulling his second tour of duty in Iraq."

"Have you told Nathan yet?"

"I did."

"And?"

"And he knows about her marriage, but she told him it is over. Nathan thinks she is waiting until her husband comes home to divorce him."

"Is she playing him?"

"I think so."

Her voice became tender, "Poor Nathan."

"I guess that complicates things with Mr. Poe, doesn't it?" Kevin stood up quickly. "Right, then my work here is done."

"Nice hair Kevin," said Nattie sarcastically.

"Yours, too." He smiled. It was his sister's habit to compliment the hairstyle of someone who had offended her rather than to offer an opinion about where that person's head might be located.

He walked to the door. "And if you would follow me to my desk, I would like to complicate things about Ms Callie."

Nattie watched over Kevin's shoulder as he brought up an article from the Asheville newspaper. The headline read: "Missing UNC-A Freshman Tennis Player." The picture was of a woman hitting a tennis ball. It could have been Callie Trainor, but the action photo made it hard to tell. The story told of a straight-A student athlete who simply disappeared instead of returning for the second semester of her freshman year. The name under the picture was Grace Lamb.

"Do you think this could be her?" asked Kevin.

"I wish the picture was better, but maybe. It is worth following up."

Kevin scrolled down and continued reading until Nattie pointed at the screen and said, "I have to go to North Carolina. Get me that girl's home address."

"What did you see?"

"Didn't you read the whole article?"

"No, why?"

"The article raises the question of a cursed dormitory room. Before this girl went missing, her roommate was killed in a car accident."

"What makes that significant?"

"Because the roommate's name was Caroline "Callie" Samms."

CHAPTER 29

MONICA LAMB

Monica Lamb was a statuesque woman, which to a height-impaired person like Nattie meant that she was not only tall but had an exaggerated sense of good posture as well. Monica was wearing a calico housedress with a small gold tennis racket hanging from a gold chain around her neck. "Come in," she said, inviting Nattie into her home without asking who she was.

"Thank you." Once she had entered the large Tudor home, Nattie stopped to gaze at the interior.

"The Lamb living room looked like a picture from a Hickory Chair brochure. A mild floral smell accented a room filled with rich wooden furniture; a large entertainment center faced a couch that did not look like it had ever been dented. Floral patterned pillows matching the window treatments were perfectly placed along the back of the couch. Wooden end tables, cabinets, and a large coffee table were placed around the room and the finishing touch was a huge oil painting of two beautiful girls, one blond and one brunette, wearing Easter dresses hanging above the couch. The blond looked like she could have been Callie Trainor.

"You have a lovely home."

Monica smiled meekly and gestured towards a hallway. "I thought we could meet in the kitchen."

The kitchen was large with state-of-the-art stainless steel appliances that all still shone like new. A breakfast counter with three captain's chairs on one side divided the room in half. A bay window overlooking a small lake filled the wall beyond the counter. Monica had Nattie sit in one of the two upholstered chairs facing the bay window.

"What a nice view," said Nattie politely.

Nattie felt guilty in Monica's presence. It was one thing to weave a story to get information about someone who was up to no good, but Monica was an innocent. Her daughter disappeared over a decade ago. She was hanging on to a thread of hope that her daughter was still alive and would one day return. Lying to Monica did not feel so justifiable.

The lie was not a horrible lie, if lies could be ranked. Nattie had told Monica that she was Twila Pierce, a feature writer from the *Bristol Herald Courier,* and that she writing a story about families of missing children.

Monica had agreed to talk on the condition of anonymity. "My husband and I have very different feelings about this. He would find this very upsetting," Monica told her on the phone.

"What would you like to know?" Monica asked as she placed two coffee mugs on the little table between the two chairs.

"First, Mrs. Lamb, I want to thank you for agreeing to meet me. I am sure talking about your daughter must be difficult."

Monica stared expressionlessly back at her.

"As I explained on the phone," continued Nattie, "I am doing a feature about families who have experienced what you have. About how they are coping and how they keep the investigation going."

Monica nodded. Her expression did not change.

"Maybe you could tell me about your daughter's disappearance," suggested Nattie. She picked up her coffee mug and took a sip, hoping it would trigger Monica's side of the conversation.

Monica faced the lake. "It was Gracie's freshman year at UNC-A. That's University of North Carolina in Asheville. She had come home for the Christmas holiday. She went back to school on the afternoon of New Year's Day. That is the last we ever saw her." Monica's voice cracked, but her face remained stoic. "A week later the school called because she had missed a number of classes and no one at her dormitory had seen her since their break."

Looking at Nattie, "I suppose you must think I am a horrible mother that I did not know she was missing sooner, but you have to understand, we are all very independent people. I'm not one of those moms who checked up on her kids all the time and Gracie isn't the kind who needs or wants that either. When I had not heard from her for a couple of days I called and left a message on her phone." [pause] ""Two days after that the school called"

"What do you think happened?"

Monica turned to Nattie. "Someone had to take her. She never would have just disappeared like that. She would never have gone anywhere without letting me know first."

Nattie was careful to avoid any sign of doubt or disagreement.

"I know you probably expected me to say that, but it is true—that is the kind of person she was."

The use of the past tense did not go unnoticed. Up until that moment Monica had always referred to her daughter in the present tense.

Monica pointed her finger upward as if getting ready to make a speech. "That is something you can put in your article. After a while, people treat you like everything you say is a cliché, like you didn't really know your daughter and your thoughts are a fantasy that make you look fragile or deluded."

Nattie reached across the table and lightly touched the woman's forearm. "For the record, Mrs. Lamb, I did not think any of those things."

Monica eyed her suspiciously for a moment before sighing again. It was the first time her expression seemed to soften. "I'm sorry," she said. "I guess that after a while it is what you expect from everyone. I haven't spoken out loud about Gracie for a couple of years." Nattie could feel Monica's forearm tighten as she made a fist. "My husband cannot handle talking about her. It is too painful for him to be reminded."

Monica suddenly stood up and wiped the corner of her eye. The movement startled Nattie. "Are you okay?"

"No, but I can pretend. That is what I can do, pretend. That is what happens to people who go through things like this."

That's what happens to people who aren't allowed to grieve, thought Nattie.

"I am sorry," Monica apologized. "I have some muffins. Would you care for a muffin?" The composed Mrs. Lamb was back.

Nattie shook her head. "No thank you."

Sitting back down, Monica stared out the window. "You wanted to know about how we kept the investigation going. For the first few weeks they talked to us every day. Then it dropped to several times a month. Then it became us calling them. We got tired of hearing 'there are no new developments.' Edward was ready to give up, but I talked him into hiring a PI. I couldn't give up. How could you give up on your daughter?" She paused and took several deep breaths. "It didn't do any good, though. After a year of that, the PI advised us to save our money.

"Save your money," Monica repeated sardonically. "So we started pretending our lives had gone on. Putting on the All-American family face." She turned to face Nattie. "And that is when we stopped trying to keep the investigation alive. So I can't tell you how we kept it going because we didn't keep it going. It was just too hard on Edward. There was a very tight bond between him and Gracie. Did you know that she went to college on a tennis scholarship?"

"I did not."

"Well, she did. She had the grades and test scores to have gone anywhere she wanted. And we could have afforded to send her anywhere, but that tennis scholarship was for her daddy. He played tennis at Elon, and he started coaching her when she was little. She was a daddy's girl. To her he hung the moon." Monica shook her head slowly and snorted. "In her eyes he could do no wrong. That is why he took their last phone conversations so badly. They had never argued before. I don't think they had ever even disagreed before."

"What did they argue about?"

"It wasn't really about Gracie. We had sponsored an exchange student from Chad. His name was Moses and he was a junior at Brevard College. He had stayed with us over that Christmas break. Gracie's car was being worked on, so they came together in his old car. Edward and I went to Anderson, South Carolina, to spend New Year's with some college friends. The girls, that is Grace and Tina, our other daughter, took Moses to a party and the next day Moses and Grace returned to school. And that is when it happened." She bit her lower lip. "Tina claimed that after Moses took Gracie to school, he came back and molested her." Monica's eyes teared up. "It was a lie, though; he didn't do it. But we believed her and called the police. They believed her story, but nothing happened after they investigated. Moses denied it and there was no evidence, so it was just her word against his. But we believed her. Edward withdrew his financial support so Moses could not stay in school. He went back home."

"I don't understand where the disagreement between your husband and daughter came in," stated Nattie.

"Gracie didn't believe her sister. She and Tina never got along well. Partly because they were so close in age—Tina was two years younger—but mostly because Tina had to live in Gracie's shadow. Grace was an excellent student and a fine athlete. She was so popular that she was in the homecoming court every year of high school and was queen her senior year, but she could have cared less about that sort of thing. Tina was a bit dramatic. I think the only way she could get attention away from her sister was to create a mini-crisis or drama. That is why Grace insisted that Tina was lying and begged her father not to send Moses home. But he was furious—we both were."

"You are saying you know Tina lied?"

Monica's face went blank again. "Tina died a little over a year ago. Medical issues. But before she did, she confessed to us that she had lied. After her passing, we moved from Asheville. Too many painful memories in that town for us."

"I am sorry," Nattie said with a tenderness she truly felt.

"Thank you," returned Monica mechanically as she began to gather herself by brushing an imaginary crumb or two from her lap and several tugs at the edges of her blouse.

Nattie knew these gestures signaled the end of their interview before Monica spoke the words.

"I'm not sure what else I could tell you."

Nattie had hoped to see some better pictures of Grace Lamb. The photo Kevin found on the Internet could be Callie Trainor, but a better picture would have helped to know for sure. Nattie was, however, hesitant to ask for a photo after all that Monica had shared.

It won't be a complete waste of my time if I can at least ask her for some pictures of Grace without sounding heartless, thought Nattie as she said, "Thank you. You have been most gracious and most helpful."

CHAPTER 30

ASHEVILLE

"How did it go?"

"I don't know Kevin. She might be Callie's mom, but I can't be sure. The pictures I saw were all too young. They could have been pictures of Callie but I don't know."

"I'm sorry. It was worth it to at least verify that it still could be her."

"Thanks. Is there a reason you wanted me to call you as soon as I started back to Bristol?"

"Yeah. You are going to come to the Asheville Airport exit pretty soon and that's where the World Market is."

"What's there?"

"There are a lot of unusual things there. I thought you might want to check it out."

And what do you want?

"And as long as you are there would you get me some chocolate?"

"Anything special or just something exotic?"

"They have their own house brand of Chocolate bars and I want the one with Chipotle Chocolate."

"Are you serious. Chocolate and chili peppers?"

"I know, it doesn't sound good but it's great, especially with coffee."

127

ater Nattie, with a Chipotle-Chocolate bar in her bag

she blurted as her ignition key failed to even elicit a ...er car.

od she tried to jiggle the battery posts but they were tig... as none of that crud around them either. One more try at the ignition , oved no different.

Turning to her next strategy she took out her phone, "Kevin, call AAA."

"What happened? Are you okay?"

"I'm fine. My car won't start."

"Maybe it's the battery."

"Kevin, just call AAA for me, I'm in the World Market parking lot."

"What did it sound like?"

"No sound at all. I turned the key and nothing happened."

"Did you check the posts on the battery? Sometimes there's loose cables and corrosion."

"There's nothing loose and there's no corrosion and I did the rain dance, so now it's time for AAA."

"I'll get you the number. You know you should just go ahead and put their number in your phone."

"Do you have the number?"

"Of course."

"Then I don't need it," she answered sharply.

"Are you mad at me?"

The question threw her off. She was not supposed to get mad. It was a rule. No one told her this rule, but it was a rule none-the-less. She knew that as an Adult Child of An Alcoholic she had grown up with the same three rules all dysfunctional family shared; don't tell, don't need, and don't feel. She knew this because her mother had taken her to Ala-Teen meetings when they first left Nattie's father in Illinois and moved to Johnson City. But knowing that the rule is there and knowing that it is dysfunctional does not keep it from being a rule. And having a "don't be angry" rule did not stop anyone from being angry. It just stopped the anger from being noticed or acknowledged.

"I'm not angry," she said weakly, "I'm just frustrated. The trip to Brevard took all day and it got me nowhere. And now my car is dead and I'm still two hours from home. So please, just call AAA. I'm going to sit in my car and read until they get here. Hopefully it will be something they can fix right away and I'll come home."

An hour and a half later she was told that her starter was bad and that they could get it to a garage, but it would not be ready until the next morning at the earliest. She would be spending the night in Asheville. As they loaded her car on their flat bed she called Kevin again.

"I'm glad you called. I just got off the phone with Monica Lamb. She called to say she remembered something that might be of interest to you."

"First things first Kevin. They say it's my starter and a new one will take until tomorrow morning."

"So you need a place to stay tonight, right?"

"Yes."

"I booked you into the Renaissance right after we talked an hour ago."

"Why did you do that Kevin?"

"I figured it was better to have the reservation and cancel it if you didn't end up needing it that to need it and it be too late to get it."

"Well done."

"You'll like the Renaissance. It's right downtown. You can walk to Salsas restaurant and there are great coffee places all over town. And, oh yeah, you are going to want to go by Sweet Mommas for a hot made to order cookie. It's right between the hotel and Salsas, just ask anyone. And get me a peanut butter chocolate chip cookie while you are there."

"Gee Kevin, you have this worked out pretty well. You didn't plan my starter going dead did you?"

"Nah. I just know Asheville very well. Soooo, now that we have that settled do you want to hear about my phone call?"

"Sure."

"After you left Mrs. Lamb remembered someone else who kept the police interested, a boy named William Aldridge. I've got his mother's name and phone number, and do you want to know what she said about young William?"

"What?"

"He was especially good with posters and pamphlets."

"Okay," she said openly confused.

"Posters and pamphlets full of pictures of her daughter."

"Pictures?"

"Yes. Lots of pictures." He paused, "Do you want me to set up a meet with William's mother tomorrow?"

"What do you think?"

"I think your evening in Asheville just got better."

As Nattie slid her pass card through the door lock on her hotel room she felt her cell phone vibrate in her pocket.

Shifting the coffee into her left hand she opened the phone with her right. It was Kevin, again, of course. The text message read; 'did u get 2 mommas before it closed?"

The question irritated her. She was still irritated at him because *a detour to get him a candy bar resulted in my starter quitting. The starter may have quit anyway. But it happened when I was getting him a candy bar.* She realized that she had been a bit rude to him when it happened. *But then she had to force him to do his job with my car. And then there is his deciding to put me in the more expensive downtown hotel.* Then again, she reasoned the stay in Asheville worked out because of the visit to Mrs. Aldridge scheduled for tomorrow morning. And the Renaissance Hotel was actually worth the extra money.

On an emotional level she was still irritated with him, but at least intellectually she knew it was unjustified …this time. She decided she would call him back, but after she got settled in. After putting the mini toothbrush and toothpaste from the front desk in the bathroom she washed her face and got as comfortable as she could using the oversized Malaprop's Bookstore tee shirt as a nightie.

After a minute to rearrange the plethora of pillows on her bed Nattie settled into bed. With her oversized decafe coffee on the night table she went through her shoulder bag on the bed next to her and withdrew the copy of *The Secret Life of Bees* she had just bought. Placing the book on her lap she scrunched back until she had the pillows just right and then she did the last thing she had to do before finishing the day off right. She called her brother.

"Hey Sarge," he answered, "are you still mad at me?"

"I not mad at you."

"Maybe just a little," he asked again in a baby voice.

"I was mad," she replied firmly, "but I'm not mad now, however I can mad in a hurry if that's what you're after."

"Easy Sarge, I'm just trying to check on you. Is your room okay?"

"Actually, it's quite nice, thank you. I was a little upset with the price, but it's probably pretty reasonable for downtown and I love that it is downtown."

"Wait a minute. I don't think I quite heard that. Did you say I got it right?"

Ignoring him she continued, "I explored the downtown a little. I found a place I'm going to have breakfast at tomorrow, the Tupelo Honey Café. I heard a guy on the sidewalk talk about the huge cathead biscuits he had there. And I had diner at that Mexican-Caribbean place you recommended."

"Salsa?"

"Yes. And it was great. And then I walked over to a bookstore the waitress told me about."

"You went to a bookstore after dinner?" he asked impatiently.

"Yes. And I bought a book and a tee shirt, is that a problem?"

"No," he said unconvincingly, "I just hope you made it to Sweet Mommas before they closed is all." He paused before adding, "You did make it there before it closed didn't you?"

"I didn't Kevin, I'm sorry, but I asked the waitress for directions and she told me they have moved. It's not downtown anymore."

"Oh man," he said in a drawn out whiney voice, "that was the whole reason I sent you there. Their cookies are the best in the world. I can't believe it."

"I'm sorry Kevin."

"I know," he answered, still whining, "I've had a long day and I was really looking forward to one of those giant peanut-butter chocolate chip numbers tomorrow."

You've had a long day, she thought before saying, "I thought you set me up downtown because you were thinking of how convenient it would be for me."

"It is convenient for you, isn't it? You just said so."

But it was more for your convenience wasn't it?

131

"Oh well," he continued in a more chipper voice, "at least I have the Chipotle-Chocolate bar from World Market."

By the time Kevin had finished speaking Nattie had fished the Chipotle-Chocolate bar. Looking at it in her hand she said, "I hate to disappoint you, Kevin, but they were all out of those candy bars."

As she went to sleep Nattie's last thought was, *you were right about that chocolate Kevin, it was great with coffee.*

CHAPTER 31

THELMA ALDRIDGE

The Aldridge home, a lovely Cape Cod in an older neighborhood, was just off Merrimon Avenue, north of the I-240 by-pass. In Asheville, an older neighborhood meant well-established trees and loads of shade. Walking towards the house, Nattie especially noticed the cool breeze underneath the canopy of foliage. Trees were missing from the yard of her Cape Cod home in Bristol.

It took Thelma better than a minute to answer the door. "Can I help you," she said, wiping her hands on her apron. She was short, the same height as Nattie, although 25 years older and 40 pounds heavier. A smudge of flour graced the tip of her nose.

"I am Twila pierce from the *Bristol Herald Courier*. I got your name from Monica Lamb."

"Oh, of course, don't mind me. I just expected someone much older. But that is just silly. Come on in and make yourself at home. My, my, aren't you a pretty one."

Nattie found herself short of breath as she listened to the energetic Thelma Aldridge.

Waving for Nattie to follow Thelma said over her shoulder, "Let's go back to the kitchen."

133

The Aldridge home could not have been more different than the Lamb home. The hallway was poorly lit by an overhead fixture that was probably not its' current shade of yellow when it was new. The tight space felt even more crowded by the random array of framed photographs on each wall, most of which were askew and two appeared to have fallen from their places and were left leaning where they landed.

"I'm making snickerdoodle cookies and I just opened a bottle of wine. Do you like red wine?"

"I do, but I better take a pass on the wine. I have to drive back to Bristol in a bit."

"Of course, I wasn't thinking. A beer then?"

Nattie looked at her silently for a moment expecting a smile or some other indication that she was joking, but the ever bubbly Thelma just stood there looking at her like she expected an answer to what she thought was a question Martha Stewart might have asked.

"No thank you. I'm fine. Can I just go ahead and ask a few questions?"

"Of course, dear. I am nothing if not an open book. I've always liked that phrase, 'an open book,' don't you?"

Inhaling slowly, Nattie asked, "Do you have a son named William? And did he establish a marathon in Grace Lamb's name?"

"Yes. That is my Billy. When he puts his mind to something, it gets done. Why, when he was in junior high school, my husband, Lucas, that's not Billy's father—his father left us when he was six—anyway, Lucas told Billy that he could not earn enough money to buy an X-box, but he did. He sure did. He never got along with Lucas, though. Bad chemistry, I think. That is why he did not let Lucas adopt him. He kept his father's name, but I don't let that bother me."

"Do you think Billy had any idea of why Grace left?"

"Did she leave? I thought she was kidnapped. So did Lucas. Billy was the one who always said she would be back."

"But did he know why she left?"

"Oh my, no. He hardly knew her at all. She was a lot older than him in school. He was just moved by her story. That's the kind of boy Billy is."

"Well then, let me thank you for your time, Mrs. Aldridge." Nattie made to leave. "Oh, could trouble you for one more thing?"

"Oh, you are no trouble, dear, no trouble at all." Thelma touched Nattie's nose with her flour-covered finger. "You are just as cute as you could be."

"I'd like a good picture of Grace Lamb, if you have one. I would have asked Mrs. Lamb for one, but I think our conversation had already upset her enough?"

"Isn't that thoughtful of you. Thoughtfulness is a dying quality these days. A picture, you say?" She grinned. "I think I can show you a picture or two. You can't take them, mind you—they belong to Billy. I can show you a picture of Grace."

"That's fine, Mrs. Aldridge. I can take a picture of a picture, if need be."

Thelma tilted her head back and drained the four ounces of red wine remaining in her glass. "Follow me," she said as she marched from the kitchen.

Nattie followed as she was told. Thelma led them down another dark hallway. The musty old-house smell was more noticeable as they got further from the kitchen.

Thelma stopped at the end of the hall and opened the door to let Nattie in. "This is Billy's room. I think you can find a picture in there somewhere."

The light was off, but Nattie could see well enough to walk to the center of the room and avoid running into the only two pieces of furniture there, a bed and a desk.

Thelma giggled as she turned on the light and Nattie's eyes grew large. She was standing in the middle of a virtual shrine to Callie Trainor, the former Grace Lamb. There had to be hundreds of pictures scattered all over the wall facing the foot of the bed; black and white and color photos of every size, including a poster of the marathon, sporting a close up of Callie's face. There were pictures of Callie playing tennis with several different hair styles, presumably taken during different tennis seasons. There were shots of her at the beach, coming out of a movie theater, and driving in a car.

Nattie asked, "Did your son take all these pictures?"

"Every single one of them," answered Thelma with pride. "He has a good eye don't you think?"

He's a stalker, thought Nattie. *He may not have known Grace Lamb, but he was taking photos of her years before she disappeared.*

Thelma took a framed picture from the desk. "Here's a picture of Grace at her senior prom. Billy used a computer and put himself in the picture with her. Did you know you could do that?"

Nattie took one look at the picture in Thelma's hand and knew she had to get back to Johnson City as soon as she could.

CHAPTER 32

BACK AT LIONEL'S OFFICE

As Nattie passed the "Welcome to Tennessee" sign, she called Lionel's office. "I will be there in half an hour. Tell him it is urgent," she told his receptionist.

Half an hour later she was being told to have a seat and wait. Before she sat down, a young man she did not know, probably a college intern came to get her. "Follow me please," he said and led her to the conference room instead of to the second floor, where Lionel's office was located.

On the other side of the conference table opposite the door, sat Callie Trainor.

"Cal—" Nattie started to say before being harshly interrupted.

"Do not say another word," ordered Greg Taylor pointing an angry finger into Nattie's face. He had been standing just inside the door so Nattie had not seen him when she entered. Now, with his body directly between she and Callie he continued to glare at her while keeping his finger in her face.

Attempting to make eye contact with Callie, Nattie tried to look around him, but he would not allow her more than a glimpse. Callie sat unmoving and hidden behind dark sunglasses.

When Nattie finally nodded, he turned towards Callie and asked, "Is this the woman who followed you to your therapist's office?"

"Yes."

Turning back to Nattie, he lifted up some papers he held in his left hand so tightly that he was nearly wading them up. "This," he said, "is a restraining order. It will be issued within the hour; and it states that if you come within fifty yards of Mrs. Trainor or attempt to make contact with her in any way—whether by phone, text, email, or any other mode of communication—you will be in violation. And—" He stepped close enough that Nattie could feel his breath. "—if you violate this, I will personally make sure you are prosecuted to the fullest extent I can. Do you understand me?"

"I understand," she said. *I understand more than you think*. "I am here to see Lionel O'Brien."

"He knows you are here; and when he is ready for you, you will know it. But for now Mrs. Trainor has requested to have a few words with you before this restraining order is put into effect."

Nattie looked at Callie, who had sat staring at her since she entered the room.

"Thank you Greg," Callie said as she stood up and began circling the table. "You can leave us now."

"Leave?" Greg asked, surprised by Callie's direction. "As your lawyer I highly recommend that you let me stay."

"That won't be necessary."

"But—"

Callie came to a stop next to her lawyer and gave him what was clearly an icy stare, even though her eyes were still hidden behind dark sunglasses. "And please shut the door."

Nattie was glad that Callie's attention had shifted from herself to Greg Taylor. She watched him carefully avoid eye contact and leave the room.

The sunglasses glared at Nattie. "You lied to me," she said as soon as she heard the door close. "You asked for my help and you lied to me. You used my good intentions to take advantage of me."

"I know I was not up front with you when I approached you at your counselor's office, but everything I said to you was true."

"Really? You told me your name was Natasha."

"Well, actually—" Nattie grinned despite herself. "I kind of am Natasha, but that is a long story. Everything I told you about my ex-husband and my family was 100% true."

"I don't care about your struggles, Natasha, or whoever you are. I did care, and you spit in my face because of it. I just wanted to look you in the eye one more time and ask how you live with it?"

"I was doing my job, Callie. I was not trying to hurt you."

"Stop right there." She took off her sunglasses, revealing bloodshot eyes. "My husband was just killed—for no reason that I know of—and you are working to free the man accused of killing him."

"That's right. Gil Peters is accused. If he did not do it, then the real killer is still out there getting away with it."

"Do you think I can sleep at night?" she asked. "I lie in bed all night long and ask myself, 'Why him? Why him?'"

"But what if Gil didn't do it?"

"What if he did? What if he did it, and you used me to get him off? How would you sleep at night then, Natasha?"

"If Gil Peters is guilty of killing your husband, then a search for the truth will not get him off. If I found out he was guilty, then I would see to it that he paid."

Callie put her sunglasses back on.

"That is how I work," Nattie said pointedly. "And that is what I told the people who hired me. If he is innocent, then he has a right to the truth. Besides, you were not willing to talk to me."

"That is ridiculous," Callie replied. Her voice was icy. "I don't believe anything you say." Turning, she began making her way back to her seat on the other side of the table.

"Just answer me this," pleaded Nattie. "Whose idea was the phony lawsuit?"

The question stopped Callie where she stood. Her head drooped as if she were debating within herself. Nattie was convinced Callie was just about to turn back around, but Greg Taylor burst back into the room.

"Lionel will see you now," Greg stated, the harshness still in his voice.

"Callie, there is more I need to tell you—" began Nattie desperately.

"That is where you are wrong Ms Moreland. You have nothing more to say," interrupted Greg.

"Callie?" Nattie called out.

Stepping between them, Greg insisted, "Mr. O'Brien is waiting."
"Nice hair, Greg," she said with a snarl.
Pointing at the door, he snarled back, "He's waiting—now."

Lionel was standing behind his desk looking out his window when Nattie entered his office. "We need to talk," she announced.

"I agree," he said solemnly. "We need to talk."

Greg Taylor, who had followed Nattie up the stairs came and stood next to Lionel's desk.

"Would you mind giving us some privacy?" asked Nattie, expecting her stepfather to back her up.

Instead of agreeing with her, Lionel reached out and took the document from Greg's hand. He looked it over quickly and handed it back to Greg while Nattie stood watching with folded arms. If she had been tapping her toe, she would have looking like an impatient schoolteacher.

"You can sit," said Greg.

"Yes Natalie, please sit," added Lionel as he came around his desk. Instead of sitting in the chair next to her, however, he stopped directly in front of her and sat back against the edge of his desk. "I cannot begin to tell you how disappointed I am."

"I'm sure you are," agreed Nattie calmly.

"I thought we had an understanding," he began. "You have violated the sanctity of a woman's grief, you have broken your word to me, and you have embarrassed me in front of my staff."

"I never agreed to stay away from Mrs. Trainor. You know as well as I do that she will have to answer questions sooner or later."

Lionel threw his head back. "That is not the point. You do not get to decide when she is to answer questions, and she gets to decide if she will answer questions with or without counsel present."

Nattie looked at Greg who was enjoying the show. "Could we please finish this conversation privately?"

"Yes, Mr. Taylor. I believe you have a document to see to, don't you?"

"Yes sir," answered Greg as he stood to attention

When she heard the door close behind her, Nattie stood up and pleadingly took hold of each of his arms. "Please, just give me two minutes," she begged.

CHAPTER 33

GREG TAYLOR GOES TO NATTIE'S OFFICE

Standing at Kevin's desk, Nattie watched Greg Taylor get out of his Mini Cooper and preen himself. He had arrived at 8:25, but waited until 8:35 to come in. "I have to be at the Bristol courthouse at 9:00," he had said when Nattie called him the previous afternoon to invite him to come by and talk to her face to face. He had agreed to meet with her without asking a single question about their meeting.

If you were going to posture before someone by making them wait, you should do it somewhere other than where they could see you. At least make it look like you were busy on the phone, thought Nattie as she watched him straighten his tie, tuck in his shirt, and adjust his pants. *Come on in, you peacock.*

The smug factor of Greg's smile was approaching "six" when he entered Nattie's waiting room. "Okay, I am here. What can I do for you?"

"There is something we need to talk about, Greg, and I think you know what it is."

"Not really," he said as he clasped his hands together behind his back and strolled leisurely around her waiting room. The smug factor of his smile rose to "eight." "Is that the original?" He pointed at her poster of *The Birth of Venus*.

Nattie feigned a smile. "I don't suppose you know anything about the meeting I had yesterday with my step-father?"

A puzzled expression crossed Greg's face, and he cocked his head to the left. "Meeting?"

"I was commanded to appear before the right honorable Lionel O'Brien, where I was told to leave Callie Oliver alone or I would be facing criminal charges."

"That must have been tough to hear from your step-father," observed Greg. Then, as he turned away from her and resumed his examination of her waiting room, he added, "I understand that you and he are real close."

"Not really," she confessed, thinking, *You've really done your homework on me, haven't you, peacock*

"That's a shame," he said casually without looking at her.

"He objected to my meeting with Mrs. Oliver under false pretenses."

Greg turned slowly to look at Nattie as if he expected her to say more. He took two steps toward her and still leaned forward trying to coax more from her.

"But meeting with her under false pretenses is not a criminal offense is it?"

"No, it's not," he admitted, "but—" He caught himself before he said more.

"But Mrs. Oliver was in Lionel's office and now she knows who I am and what I was doing."

"We told you to stay away from our client, Ms McMorales." He raised his eyebrows. "You were warned."

"I was warned," admitted Nattie. "And now I've been ordered to apologize to you."

Greg stopped leaning forward and straightened up, the way you would when you finally heard what you were listening for. His smile reached "ten" on the smug scale. "So that's what this meeting is about? You have to confess to me to keep daddy happy."

Nattie ignored the jab, but waited until Greg's eyes again met hers. "You're right about my step-father. He was not happy with me when he found out that I had deceived your client."

Greg's shrug said, 'What did you expect?'

"So I am apologizing to you. And I'm dropping the investigation of Callie Oliver, too," continued Nattie. "But not for the reasons you might think."

Greg's smile lessened and his eyelids closed slightly as he cocked his head a bit to the right. "What do you mean?"

"I mean, I don't think Callie Oliver had anything to do with her husband's murder."

"Of course she didn't have anything to do with it. We know who did it. We've known who did it from the beginning. The case against him is clear." Greg threw his right hand up like he was tossing confetti into the air and then turned his back to her. "We've known who did it from the very beginning."

"The case against him is very strong, but it isn't air tight."

"Whatever you say, Ms McMorales." Greg snickered. "Whatever you say."

"Well, I say he didn't do it." Nattie paused until he stopped moving. "I say I know who did do it."

Greg turned to face her.

"Do you want to hear my theory?"

"I don't care what your theory is as long as you leave my client alone."

"The police believe that Gil Peters murdered Vince Oliver because his lawsuit was going badly. They believe Gil arranged to meet Vince at that bar because it was so remote and dark that there would be no witnesses." She took a deep breath and leaned forward. "But there was a witness."

Greg's eyelids narrowed.

"I talked to that bartender. He said Vince and Gil were together at the bar for forty minutes, and they acted like old friends who hadn't seen each other in years."

Greg's expression relaxed again.

"According to Gil Peters, their counter-lawsuits were nothing more than a publicity stunt to promote both their novels."

"We've been through that. It's old news. Mr. Peters is just trying to save his butt."

"But there is new information."

Greg sat down on the couch and spread his arms out. "Okay, Natasha, let's hear the new information."

144

"The counter lawsuits weren't Gil's idea; they were Norris's idea."

"But Mr. Peters filed the first suit. That's a documented fact."

"Also Norris's idea."

Leaning back, Greg folded his leg. "Gil Peters can say anything he wants about all that. It doesn't mean anything because he murdered the only other person who could corroborate his story."

"But there was another person involved, wasn't there?"

"How would I know that? I wasn't involved until after Mr. Peters filed his suit."

"Here's the thing, Greg. Norris Trainor didn't come up with that scheme by himself."

"No?"

"No. According to Callie, Norris did not have that kind of mind. That's why she was so sure that Gil was lying when he said it wasn't his idea."

"He was lying."

"I don't think so. I think the counter-suits were a promotion sham and I don't think either one of them came up with the idea. I think it was someone else's."

"Okay, Natasha, humor me. Is it me?" The smug expression returned.

"Yes," she said with a cool firmness intended to communicate her resolve.

They locked eyes for a long moment before Greg broke the silence. "I don't suppose you thought of how childish this accusation will look to Lionel when you tell him." He sneered and shook his head. "He'd certainly never think that this was your way to get even with me for telling him about you and Callie?" The words dripped with sarcasm.

"It's not what Lionel will think, Greg. It's what Callie will think."

Greg gathered his arms and scooted forward to the edge of the couch.

"It's a strange thing, Greg," Nattie continued. "Before Callie and Norris got married she worked for the president of National University Law School."

"Okay. What's so strange about that?"

"Right after she got married, the president's office was ransacked."

"And?"

"And the only thing taken from his office was Callie's personnel file."

"So what does any of that mean?"

This was Nattie's turn to become nonchalant and throw invisible confetti into the air. "I'm not sure what it means, but it is strange because— Where did you say you went go to law school?"

"I didn't."

Nattie smiled. "No, you didn't. It was National, wasn't it?"

"It was National. But that's nothing more than a coincidence." He pointed at her and through clinched teeth he threatened, "I'm going to warn you right now. If you are going to accuse me of something here, then you'd better be able to prove it."

Tightening her eyes and taking a quick half-step towards him had the surprise effect on him that she wanted. He retreated. "How about this for proof. The first time we met, you told me that the police had informed you of Gil Peters' claim that the lawsuits were phony." She stopped leaning towards him and added, "But he never told that to the police. He was convinced that he would get himself and Norris in trouble if he let that secret out. You see, he was still looking out for Norris' interest. So I asked myself, how would you know that he would claim the suits were a sham? No lawyer would participate in a bogus lawsuit and risk being disbarred. No, neither of them would have told you, Greg. So do you know what I think?"

"I couldn't care less what you think," he replied mustering what little bravado he could. "I only care what you can prove."

Having already tested his steel, Nattie could shrug and smile sweetly in the face of his threat. "You're right, of course. I can't prove that you knew about the fake lawsuit. And I can't prove that you stole Callie's personnel file. What I can prove is that you have been obsessed with Callie Trainor for a long time."

Greg's breathing got heavy enough to hear.

"Or maybe I should say that you've been obsessed with Cassie Lamb for a long time. Isn't that right, William?"

Greg's eyes flashed as he tried, unsuccessfully, to hide his building rage.

"I've been to your mother's house in Asheville, William. I've seen the shrine to Cassie in your bedroom." She watched the veins in his neck pop out and his jaw throb before adding in an even sweeter voice, "You know William, you really should call your mother more often. She really worries about her Billy."

Throwing his head back, Greg let out a scream. It was the kind of scream that junior high school boys use just before they attack someone. Maybe the scream is supposed to frighten their victims, or maybe it is to gather enough courage to go through with the attack. Whatever the purpose, the effect of this scream was that it tipped Greg's hand. Leaping to his feet, he charged at her with both arms reaching for her throat. With that much warning, Nattie was ready to side-step the clumsy attack. Grabbing Greg's left wrist she knocked him off balance with her hip; and with her right arm under his armpit, she easily used his own momentum to throw him into the wall behind her.

Nattie had not anticipated that her throw would flip Greg so dramatically, but it did. As he flew by her, he was able to snag her left wrist with his right hand and pull her off balance, too. Just before he hit the wall he pulled her across himself, smashing her face first into the wall to his right. The fall loosened her hold on his wrist, allowing him to get his hands around her neck from underneath her.

From the upper position Nattie wedged her arms inside his, loosening his grip on her throat. With the heels of her hands, she began pushing his head further and further back until he let go and began thrashing from side to side, trying to wriggle out from under her.

Something like "I hate you" came from Greg's throat, but it was barely understandable because of the awkward position he was in. He resorted to a gurgling snarl as he trashed under Nattie's weight. This stalemate continued until he realized that they were not alone.

"Greg." It was Callie's voice. Callie Trainor, Lionel O'Brien, and a Johnson City police office named Alan Poe had all emerged from Nattie's back office when the struggle began. Following Nattie's instructions, they waited for William Gregory Taylor to incriminate himself. The wait ended, however, when the scuffle started.

When he saw Callie, Greg stared at her in disbelief. His hands dropped to the floor, and he lay there virtually motionless. If he were aware of anyone else in the room besides Callie, he did not show it. He did not notice Nattie taking her weight off him or that the police officer, who had circled around behind him, was raising him to his feet. Greg's eyes were fixed on Callie, who stared back at him stoically. Neither of them said anything.

Greg remained passive as the officer pulled his hands behind him and placed them in handcuffs. He spoke again. "Cassie," he pleaded. "I can explain. Please."

"Mr. Taylor, I am placing you under arrest for the murder of Norris Trainor...."

Oblivious to what was being said, Greg struggled to move towards Callie, but the officer restrained him. "Please, Cassie, you have to listen to me."

"No," she said firmly. "I don't." Turning to Nattie and pointing at Greg Taylor, she asked, "Why him?" Then, while Greg was being informed of his Miranda rights, she turned and left the room without looking back.

CHAPTER 34

AFTER CALLIE LEAVES

Officer Poe helped Greg Taylor get to his feet as Nattie and Lionel watched. The arrogance was now gone from the young lawyer, replaced by a frightened wide-eyed confusion. He looked lost.

Lionel, standing shoulder to shoulder by Nattie waited until Greg had regained his footing, "I'd say you are going to need a good lawyer, Gregory."

Greg sighed. Relaxing his shoulders, neck, and jaw, "Oh, thank you, Lionel, sir. I appreciate that."

"You may consider that free advice, young man," Lionel replied, "not an invitation."

"Let's go," said Alan Poe as he turned the shocked Greg Taylor towards the door. Leading his prisoner by the left arm, Alan reached the door, hesitated, and looked back at Nattie. She crossed the room and stopping in front of him she stood on her toes to kiss him on the cheek. Even then he had to lean forward a bit.

"Thank you, Alan. You have been a huge help. I know you are here on your day off, too."

He grinned. "It was fun to be here while you pulled all of this together. It was like being inside a detective movie."

Nattie smiled.

"Can I call you?" he asked tentatively.

It was the moment she had anticipated with dread. She put her hand tenderly on his upper arm. "I wish I could accept your offer Alan, I really do. I think I really blew it in high school when I didn't say yes. But as it turns out, I am still in love with my husband. My ex-husband."

A thin smile crossed his face. "I understand. As usual, my timing is way off."

"I think it is my timing that is way off, Alan," she corrected him.

His eyes softened a moment. Then he turned towards Lionel. With a nod he said, "Sir."

Lionel nodded back, "Officer."

"Let's go." Alan led his prisoner out of the building.

Nattie stood still, watching him go. She did not notice her stepfather come up next to her until he put his arm around her. "Did I just hear you say you were in love with Nathan?"

She did not pull away from him or flinch at his touch. "You did, but don't get too excited about it. He's dating someone." *A married someone.*

"I'm sorry," he said. "Nathan must be a bigger fool than I thought he was."

She looked up at him. "Thank you. That was sweet."

He looked embarrassed.

"And thank you for believing me."

"On that account, I fear I have been remiss. I'm sorry."

"But you really came through for me when it counted. It means a lot to me. Thank you," she said tip-toeing a kiss towards his cheek.

"I'm proud of you." He leaned forward to offer his cheek.

CHAPTER 35

LONDON

London was waiting just where she said she would be, by the baggage claim area at the TriCities Airport. With long black hair and glassy blue eyes, she hardly looked her age. She was oblivious to the two college-aged guys, one wearing a UT shirt and the other in a King College shirt, who kept glancing in her direction.

Ease off boys, thought Nattie. *She's older than your mothers.*

When she saw Nattie approaching, she hopped up from where she was sitting and gestured a thumbs up towards Nattie. Nattie had called her the night before and told her that she knew who the real murderer was and would hopefully arrange an arrest the next morning. London had insisted on flying from Nashville and going with Nattie when she went to tell the good news to her daughter and son-in-law. She was not absolutely sure that it was settled until she saw Nattie raise her two thumbs. With that confirmation her face lit up, and she walked quickly towards Nattie. Nattie noticed the slight limp from the ankle injury London received during a 5K run in her 20's. No one who did not already know that the limp was there would have noticed. Certainly the college boys who were craning the necks to watch her embrace Nattie did not notice the limp.

"I can't believe you did it Natasha," said London. She stepped back. "I knew you could do it. And you did it." Hugging Nattie again, she went on, "But I can't believe you did it."

London's exuberance was understandable, but excessive praise always made Nattie uncomfortable. And it did not take much for her to consider it excessive. She funneled her embarrassment into an icy glare over London's shoulder at the college boys who were not even attempting to mask their stares. Neither boy caught Nattie's glare right away. The one in the King College shirt noticed finally and backhanded his friend who reacted as if he had just been woken up.

Trance time is over guys.

"I don't know how to thank you enough, Natasha; my family and I will forever be beholding to you."

"I'm just glad it worked out. For a while there I wasn't sure. If you hadn't convinced me to continue I would have given it up as a lost cause a long time ago."

Eyeing Nattie, "That would have been tragic."

"It would have." They smiled at each other for a moment before Nattie suggested, "Why don't we get your bag and get over there."

London retrieved a shoulder bag from under the seat on which she had been sitting. "I'm ready. Let's go."

"That's it?" asked Nattie pointing at the single piece of luggage.

London smiled. "It's all I had time to pack after you called last night. I'll probably only stay one night anyway. I want to give them time to get used to the idea of all this being over."

As they walked to the parking lot, London took Nattie's arm. "While I waited for you to get here, I called your office and told Kevin to add another three days to the final bill he sends to Ralph." Kevin had been submitting weekly bills to Ralph Southerland, as he had insisted.

"Three days extra? You don't need to tip me, London."

"I know."

Nattie eyed her suspiciously. "Ralph doesn't know about it does he?"

"As a matter of fact, it was his idea."

"Really?"

"Well," she smiled, "an extra day was his idea. But he would have paid $100,000 for this if he needed to."

"Well thank you. Thank you both." Then, leaning towards London, Nattie asked, "Are you sure he'll be okay with this?"

"You worry too much, young lady."

"And you're not going to tell him what you've done, are you?"

"That, my dear, is entirely between him and me."

"I feel a little guilty that you waited for me to tell the kids that it's over, but I can't help being glad that I get to be there when you do."

"There's no call for guilt, London. I was not going to tell them it's over until I was absolutely sure that it's over."

She could feel London's eyes on her, but she did not look. "I'm absolutely sure that we have the real killer now."

"So what's the problem?"

"The problem is that until they know they have an solid case against the other guy they aren't going to cut Gil loose." Glancing at London, "That's what I want to be sure of before I tell them it's over."

London waved her hand, "That's just details. It's over. I can feel it in my bones."

Nattie smiled, "Okay, with the exception of some details it's over." Then with more emphasis, "But those details are what will determine when the case against Gil is dropped."

"Details, details," London sounded like a schoolgirl. "So tell me. What is the real story? Why did Gil's friend get murdered?"

"I'm sure that there are details that I don't know but I think I've got a good grip on the basics. It was basically about a woman, Norris' wife, Callie. Norris was murdered in order to get him out of the way."

"Oh my goodness, do you mean he didn't do anything other than marry a woman someone else wanted?"

"That's it in a nutshell."

"He's Uriah all over again."

"Uriah?"

"Bathsheba's husband Uriah. When David saw her he was so blinded by his desire for her that he sent her husband off to get killed."

Nattie shook her head, "It's an old story all right. In this version the murderer went to school with the woman. She was a prom queen and he was probably a dork, and a younger dork to boot. Anyway, he had stalked her for years, taking pictures of her all over the place. That's how

153

I finally figured out that it was him, I visited his mother's home and she showed me his bedroom. It was a shrine to Callie."

"And that's how you knew he killed Norris?"

"Well, that was one of the last pieces of the puzzle. You see, sometime during her freshman year of college Callie disappeared. Actually, Callie is her alias. Her real name is Grace."

Nattie paused to breathe and to glance at London to see if she was still interested in the story and all it's details.

"What happened?"

"Well, like I said, I'm not sure of all the details, but it's not so much a David and Bathsheba story as it's a version of …. Who was the guy who went to prison because he was falsely accused of molesting that King's wife?"

London looked down for a moment, "Do you mean Joseph and Potiphar's wife?"

"Maybe. That's sounds like it could be right."

"So what happened?"

"I'm not sure, but whatever it was made her so upset that she broke all ties with her past. She changed her name and went to Washington, DC. She ended up working at a law school, and it just so happened that it was the same law school where the stalker was a student."

Gasping, "Are you serious, it's a lawyer?"

"He was a law student at the time, but yes, he's a lawyer. He's their lawyer, but that's getting ahead of the story."

"I'm sorry. Go ahead."

"Well, right after Callie got married and left that job her records were stolen."

"The lawyer?"

"Probably. All we know is that when I went to check on her background they discovered her personnel file was missing. So we don't have a way to know how long they were missing, but when I mentioned it to her former boss he remembered that right after she left, his office was ransacked and the only thing missing was his address book. He didn't connect it to her until he and I started putting the pieces together."

"Wow," shaking her head, "the poor girl. He hunted her down and she had no idea."

"She didn't." They drove rode silently for a few miles before Nattie continued, "I don't know how he did this, but somehow he managed to get himself into the position of Norris' lawyer."

"That's scary."

"It is. Norris trusted him. He didn't have a reason to not trust him. As near as I can tell it was the lawyer's idea for these two writers to sue each other for libel."

"Isn't that illegal for a lawyer to encourage a client to do something illegal."

"If it isn't it should be," agreed Nattie, "but either way he convinced Norris to act like it was his idea. Under the guise of keeping his countersuit suggestion hidden he got Norris to keep his real agenda hidden."

"Do you mean that those countersuits were just a cover for his killing Norris?"

"Yes."

"That means he was intending to frame Gil from the very beginning."

"Yes."

London stared out the front window with her mouth open.

"Incredible, isn't it?"

Looking back at Nattie, "What kind of a sick twisted mind thinks of something like that?"

"He's probably a genius."

"A sick twisted genius."

"Yes."

Touching Nattie's arm, "Oh my, and he had it all planned so that he was there in place to comfort the grieving widow."

"Like we said, it was an ingenious plan."

Tightening her grip on Nattie arms a bit, "But you outsmarted him."

"I got lucky."

"And you not only saved Gil." She paused until Nattie glanced at her, "But you saved that poor woman too."

CHAPTER 36

GILL PETERS IS EXONERATED

As they got closer to Johnson City, Nattie called Alan Poe for an update on Gil Peters' status.

"He is still in the interrogation room, but it is a formality. The little creep has spilled his guts already, so it's just a matter of getting the details to the District Attorney so she can get the paperwork done. As soon as the paperwork on Mr. Taylor is processed, I will make sure that your guy gets cleared."

"Thanks, Alan."

"Of course, and Nattie, thank you. This is going to speed up getting my detective shield."

"I'm happy for you, Alan. I really am. And I'm sorry I misjudged you in high school."

"Maybe next time I ask you out it will be different."

Nattie turned her head towards the window, hiding her grin from London. *I don't think so Alan, but thank you.*

Natalie Peters looked awful as she opened the door. As a younger version of her mother, she would normally be very attractive; but the worry and stress were wearing on her. Hair unkempt, no makeup, swollen eyes, washed-out complexion, and a lime green sweat suit that did not match the fire-engine-red bandana that held her hair—it took her a moment to recognize who was at her door. The crease between her eyebrows deepened as she closed and then reopened her eyes.

"Mother?" she asked as if she needed to hear an answer before she would believe her eyes.

London stepped through the door and embraced her daughter. "I'm sorry to drop in unannounced like this, baby girl. I just had to bring you the news in person."

"News?" she asked, looking first at Nattie then back at her mother.

"You tell her, Natasha," instructed London.

Natalie looked to Nattie with a pitiful expression. London and Nattie had believed that if their presence was not enough to confirm the good news, surely their smiles would do it. But Natalie's hope was spent. She'd have to be absolutely sure the news was good before she would let go of any more of her caution.

Nattie assumed as calm a voice as she could muster. "They arrested Greg Taylor for the murder of Norris Trainor this morning."

Natalie's face remained blank. She slowly turned from Nattie to look for affirmation from her mother.

"That's right. Gil will be exonerated."

The beginnings of a smile crept across Natalie's face. "Exonerated?" She repeated the word timidly.

"Well, there will be some paperwork to get through before everything's legal; but it's official. The murderer was arrested this morning and I got the call that he confessed while I was bringing your mother from the airport."

A pinkish glow emerged on Natalie's face, which grew more and more animated. "Does Gil know?"

"We thought you'd like to tell him," replied London.

"He'll be here in an hour." Natalie pulled the bandana from her head and patted her hair. "I've got to get cleaned up." She looked back and forth between her two visitors. "I don't have anything for dinner."

"Why don't you get yourself ready," said London, "and we'll go pick something up for dinner. It that okay with you, Natasha?"

"Absolutely, what's his favorite place?"

"The Thai place over by Barnes and Noble."

"The Stir Fry Cafe?"

Natalie nodded.

"I know right where it is. What do you want us to get?"

"We both love the chicken Pad Ped."

Nattie pulled her keys from her pocket. "We'll be back in forty-five minutes."

Fifty-five minutes later they arrived back at the Peters' home with three orders of Pad Ped—a curry dish with peanuts, potatoes, and coconut milk—and some chicken tenders for London. Natalie was still upstairs. A bottle of Vino Nobile di Montepulciano and four wine glasses sat in the middle of the dining room table.

"Hey," Nattie blurted out, "I know this wine. I was there in Montepulciano right before I met you in Florence last year."

"I remember," London called out from the kitchen, where she was placing their food in the oven to keep it warm. "I've been there, too. I had a case of that sent to the children from Italy. Gil loves it. That's probably why Natalie picked that out for the occasion. Go ahead and open it; let it breathe."

As Nattie did so, Natalie entered the room. "Oh good, I forgot to do that. Thank you." Natalie looked like a different person. Her hair was pulled back in a ponytail; and although she wore only a trace of makeup, her face had regained its color, mostly because of her own radiance. The puffiness remained under her eyes, but there was a renewed life in them that had not been there earlier. She was ecstatic, but understandably eager for her husband to get home. "I think I need a glass of that now."

Natalie's plan was for the three women to wait for Gil to discover them behind the dining room table decorated with his favorite food and his favorite wine. "He'll know it's over when he sees us with this feast."

You didn't, observed Nattie to herself as she noticed London had already opened and was pouring the wine.

"To Natasha McMorales." London lifted her wine glass in a toast. "The International Private Eye."

"I'll drink to that." Natalie tapped her mother's glass with her own. After a sizable swallow she put her glass down and hugged Nattie. "I've been so excited that I forgot to thank you."

"Seeing you this excited was more than thanks enough."

"Hello!" came Gil's voice from the front of the house. "Is everything okay? There's a car in the drive…" He did not finish his sentence as he rounded a corner and came to see the carefully orchestrated scene in the dining room.

Natalie had given them explicit instructions. "Just look natural, like you just happened to come by, and let him figure it out in his own time. Believe me, it won't take him long."

London and Nattie did as they were told. Slight smiles, like they were glad he was home; but not big ones, like he just won the lottery—or better. Natalie, however, could not follow through with her own plan. She held her hands together just below her chin and bounced like a five-year-old with a full bladder. Before he could finish his sentence, she rushed around the table. "They found the killer. They found the killer."

Just like his wife an hour earlier, Gil did not seem to be able to process what he had just heard. He looked at London and then at Nattie, who confirmed what Natalie had said with synchronized nods.

He stared across the table while his wife loosely held him and jumped up and down in excitement. He looked as if he was going to faint; instead, he just dropped to his knees. Holding his face with both his hand, he began to weep.

"It's over, Gil," said Natalie softly. She knelt and pulled his head to her. "It's finally over."

Their intimacy was captivating but quickly Nattie felt awkward watching. She turned towards London, who signaled her to the kitchen.

"Let's leave them alone," London whispered. "I'll buy dinner if you drive."

"And I'll by dinner if you'll eat something spicy."

"It's a deal, then." London left a note for Gil and Natalie on the dry marker board hanging on their kitchen wall. It read, "Gone to dinner with Natasha—be back later."

"So that means you're going to eat something spicy?" asked Nattie.

London shook her head. "No. It means I'm buying."

As they quietly closed the front door behind them, they could still hear soft weeping from the other room.

CHAPTER 37

A REUNION IN ASHEVILLE

Callie had reluctantly agreed to visit her mother provided that Nattie agree to several conditions; including that Nattie do the driving. As they passed through Sam's Gap from Tennessee into North Carolina Callie reminded Nattie of her conditions. "If I say it's time to go, we go, no questions asked."

Nattie nodded.

"I'm sorry." Callie's voice grew softer. "I don't know why I'm so on edge. I've crossed over the mountain and just driven around Asheville many times."

Nattie just smiled and nodded again.

As they descended from the state line, Route 26 turned and a beautiful landscape opened up before them. It appeared as if they were driving out of a valley towards another series of mountains in the far distance.

"This is my favorite scene," Callie mused. "When I drive out of that last turn and the panorama of those mountains over there opens up, I know I'm getting close to home. I have a photo of it hanging in my house."

"I remember." Nattie also remembered how Billy Taylor had nearly revealed his association with Asheville when she first met him in Callie's foyer.

With Nattie watching awkwardly, Callie and her mother hugged each other as if they were afraid to let go lest they lose one another again. Callie's mother had rushed out into the yard as Callie and Nattie climbed the stairs leading to the landing in front of the house. Monica Lamb then ushered them through the front door, but stopped in the foyer and placing her hands on either side of Callie's arms. She drank her daughter in with her eyes. Neither woman said anything for a long ten seconds as Monica's eyes pooled up and Callie, for the first time since Nattie had known her, looked unnerved.

"Oh sweetheart," Monica blurted out and once again drew her daughter close.

Burying her face in her mother's neck, Callie replied, "I'm sorry, Momma."

After what seemed like several minutes, Monica turned her attention to Nattie, who was standing directly behind Callie. Extending her left hand towards Nattie she held tight and smiled at her.

They squeezed hands. Callie did not move.

Beckoning Nattie to follow with her left hand, Monica kept her right arm around Callie and maneuvered her towards the living room. Nattie would have desperately preferred to excuse herself and to leave them to their private reunion, but Callie's conditions for this meeting had been explicit. By contract, Nattie was to make all the arrangements for the meeting, including the stipulation that it take place when Mr. Lamb was out of town. She had agreed to stay with Callie for the entire meeting, which was to last no more than ninety minutes, "no matter how unnecessary it might become we are going to leave in no more than an hour and a half."

"I need you there," Callie had told her, "because my mother will try to get me to make peace with my father. I don't think I have the energy or strength to deal with very much right now, so I need you to block any decision, no matter how trivial, that she asks me to make about seeing my father, coming back, or staying longer than we agreed."

Nattie had agreed, but Callie must not have been convinced because she continued, "I'm serious, I want you to swear it as one broken-heart to another."

Having never heard such an oath before Nattie had asked, "Just what is the penalty for breaking a vow of one broken heart to another?"

"Living with the knowledge that you had done it," was Callie's answer.

Nattie took the oath.

"Please sit down, Ms McMorales." Monica motioned to a chair. Then she took a seat next to Callie on the couch. "Can I get you something to drink? She pointed to the pitcher and glasses on the coffee table in front of her. We have sweet tea or I can make a pot of coffee."

"That's very kind, Mrs. Lamb. Thank you. But I'm fine right now."

"Well, just let me know if you change your mind."

Nattie smiled politely and mouthed "Thank you." She took a deep breath. The meeting was no more than five minutes long, and Nattie's protection already looked unnecessary. She would have to honor Callie's contract, but it now looked as if it was going to be the easiest money she would ever earn.

Turning to face Callie, who had not taken her eyes off of her mother since they had sat down, Monica reached out to hold her hands. "I am so sorry to hear about the loss of your husband, Gracie."

"Thank you."

"I wish I knew what to say about him, but I don't know anything about him."

"I know mother. I'm sorry—"

"Please don't apologize, Sweetheart. I didn't say that to make you feel guilty. I just wanted to explain why I don't even know enough to ask about him."

"What would you like to know, Momma?"

Monica thought a moment before asking, "Was he good to you?"

Callie smiled. It was a good question. "Yes, he was. Very good." And for the next half hour Callie told her mother about her husband, their courtship, and their marriage.

"He sounds like he was a good man."

"He is, Momma; he is."

Monica turned to Nattie. "And I think you told me that they have arrested the man who killed him. Is that right, Ms McMorales?"

"Yes it is," Callie interrupted, "and Nattie is the one who made it happen."

Monica raised her eyebrows slightly as she kept her gaze on Nattie.

"That's true, but you played a big part in solving it, Mrs. Lamb," Nattie said.

"Me? How did I help?"

"You were the one who alerted me to that boy who did all the fundraisers for Callie. I mean, Gracie."

"It's Callie, please. I haven't been Gracie for a long time."

Gasping slightly, Monica's shoulders flinched upward, she bit her lip, and then tried to mask her pain by asking, "What did Billy Aldridge have to do with this?"

"Look Momma, I know how this must hurt you, but I started a new life as Callie. I'm Mrs. Callie Trainor now. I can't go back now."

Monica stared through puddles of tears straining to say, "I just want to know that we can go forward."

"I want that too." Reaching out to wipe her mother's cheek, "We just need to go slow." Leaning closer she added, "Okay?"

Monica smiled meekly and nodded. After wiping her own cheek, "Tell me about Billy Aldridge?"

"Billy Aldridge is who killed Norris, Momma," explained Callie.

The harshness of Callie's answer widened Monica's eyes. She looked pleadingly at Nattie as if she wanted to be told she did not hear what she just heard. Finding no help in Nattie's face she looked back at Callie and asked, "He did that?"

"He did."

"I can't believe it?"

Callie watched her mother struggle to digest this revelation before changing the subject, "Tell me about Sissy."

Monica let go of Callie's hand, patted it, and then folded her hands in her lap.

"It was ovarian cancer that finally took her, but she was lost to us almost as long as you were Gracie—I mean Callie."

"You can still call me, Gracie, Momma." Patting her mother's left hand, "I just don't want you to expect me to stop using the name my husband knows me by."

Looking down Monica placed her right hand on top of Callie's hand. She nodded.

"What do you mean Sissy was lost to you?"

Monica swallowed hard and looked back down at her hands. "Sissy got into a lot of trouble after you left. She became more withdrawn and irritable. She stopped playing volleyball. I don't know when she started drinking; but after her second DUI, she was arrested for having some cocaine in her car with her."

"On my goodness. What happened?"

"Your father hired Henry Davis, who got the charges dropped on some kind of legality."

"No. I mean what happened to get all that started?"

"Oh, that's just part of it. She had three miscarriages with three different men. She didn't even know who the last one was."

"Was it the drugs?" asked Callie.

Monica slowly rubbed the palms of her hands up and down her thighs twice before answering. "We thought the drugs were a symptom of the rape."

Callie stiffened suddenly.

Noticing Callie pull away, Monica reached out and took her hand again. "I know you didn't believe she was raped, and you were right. She wasn't, but we believed her then."

Callie let her mother take her hand, but did not relax.

"Oh Gracie, I wish I could do it all over again. Both of us do, but at the time it was Moses' word against the word of our daughter. How could we not believe our daughter?"

"I knew she was lying. I told you she was lying."

"I know."

"Moses would never do what she accused him of doing."

"We took our daughter's side. What else could we have done?"

"You could have turned the case to over to the police and let them investigate."

"We did take her to the police. She filed a report about it."

Callie raised her voice in anger. "But you didn't wait to find out the truth. Daddy withdrew his support and his visa sponsorship, and Moses had to go back to Chad."

"I know."

"Did you know that Moses' brother was working in western Sudan? That's the Darfur region where there's a lot of violence. Moses went there to find his brother and got killed."

Monica looked shocked. "How do you know that, Gracie?"

"I went to Chad to find him. In fact, I've been on mission trips to Darfur three times. We owe it to Moses, Momma. We killed him."

Monica's hands went to her mouth. "Oh my goodness. That's why you disappeared, isn't it. You blamed us for his death."

Callie just stared at her mother.

"We didn't know the truth. We really didn't. We thought that all of Sissy's drugs and promiscuity were because she had been raped, but the truth was that she was dealing with the horrible guilt for having lied. She told us the truth just before she died." The tears were flowing freely now. "It nearly killed your father. He hasn't been the same since you left, and then finding out that Sissy lied broke his heart even more."

Callie reached out to hold her mother's hand; but when Monica said, "He really wants to see you," she pulled back again and looked at Nattie through wide eyes.

Nattie made a move to stand. "It is time for us to leave, Mrs. Lamb."

"No," pleaded Monica. She reached for Callie's hand, but her daughter had already moved beyond reach. "Can't you stay just a little longer? There's so much more we have to talk about. Please."

Callie looked to Nattie again.

"Thank you very much for the hospitality," said Nattie. She tried to shake hands with Monica who had become frozen in disbelief.

"When can you come back? Can we come visit you? Can I come visit you? Where do you live? Would you at least give me your phone number?" Monica's questions came in rapid succession.

"I'm afraid she can't commit to anything today, but we have your phone number. If there is to be another meeting, one of us will call you to set it up." *I was wrong. This is the hardest money I've ever had to earn.*

It took five minutes to get from the porch to the car; but true to her plan, Callie never said another word to her mother. She kept her silence until they were well on the other side of Asheville and once again on Route 26.

"Do you think I'm being unreasonable?" asked Callie.

"It's not for me to say."

Callie looked out the passenger side window. "My mother thinks I'm being unreasonable."

"Probably."

She studied Nattie. "Yes, probably. I would too if I were her. But you have to understand, all she ever wants is to make everything nice for everyone."

"There are worse things to want."

"That may be, but the problem with my mother is that she would believe whatever my father told her and do whatever kept the peace for him."

Nattie glanced at her.

Callie sneered venomously. "My father is a fraud. A fraud and a hypocrite."

Nattie glanced at her again.

"When I was a little girl, he was my hero. He taught me to treat everyone with respect until they lost it. He taught me to look past skin color, religion, or nationality to the character of a person's heart and deeds. He read 'Letter from a Birmingham Jail' to me when I was in grade school and bought me a poster of the 'I have a dream' speech when I graduated from junior high." She paused and turned her head in the other direction. Nattie watched her wipe something from her cheek. "But let a black man be accused of touching my lily-white sister and all that went out the window."

Callie did not speak again until her shoulders stopped trembling. "I didn't know Simone—that's Sissy's real name—I didn't know she had gone to the police. I'd give anything to know what she told them."

"Really?" asked Nattie. "What if I told you that I have a copy of that police report in my trunk."

Callie nearly jumped at her.

"I'll find a place to get off the road and get it for you."

Nattie pulled into the parking lot of the scenic view halfway between Asheville and Johnson City and retrieved her briefcase from the trunk of her Subaru. They sat at a picnic table while Callie read the three-page police report. When she had finished, she banged her fist on the table and then pointed at the document. "This proves Moses was innocent. Simone claimed that he came to her room on the night of New Years day." She slammed her fist down again. "She was home alone while Moses took me back to my dorm room at UNC Asheville. He was supposed to go on to Brevard, but she said he circled back because he knew my parents wouldn't be home until the next day."

Callie paused and seemed to search for some note of recognition in Nattie's face before explaining, "Moses could not have circled back to our house because he spent the whole night with me." She shook her hands back and forth. "We just talked. We sat in the lobby of my dorm and spent the whole night talking about everything from politics to religion. He told me about his family and his dream of becoming an engineer and returning home to Chad. He was going to design wells to bring clean water to the bush. We talked until the sun came up and then we went out for breakfast. After that, he took me back to my school and then drove on to his. By the time he left me, my folks were back home themselves."

"You were his alibi."

"I was."

Time slowed down to a near halt as Callie looked away, lost in her own awareness. "I was his alibi. All he had to do was tell them he was with me." Turning back to face Nattie with a frantic wild-eyed expression, "I would have told them he was with me."

"Did he tell anyone that he was with you?"

Callie's eyes grew larger. "I don't think he did— Oh my goodness. He was protecting me. He didn't tell anyone I was his alibi because he thought it would make me look bad." Her eyes turned red. "That would be just like Moses."

Callie folded her arms on the table and buried her face in them. For the third time since they met, Nattie heard Callie ask, "Why him?"

The End, Not

PLEASE ENJOY THIS BRIEF EXCERPT FROM
THE NEXT NATASHA McMORALES MYSTERY

WHY ME?

A THIRD NATASHA McMORALES MYSTERY

By C S Thompson

PROLOGUE

It was a little thing but it disappointed him anyway. He wanted to hear the 'tink' sound as he threw the empty beer can on the floor behind the passenger seat of his Mustang. You could never hear the 'tink' sound after the first beer because there was nothing for it to hit against, but with each empty can the chances of hearing the 'tink' sound got better and better. He shrugged. It was his second beer, which meant that it would have had to hit the first empty to make the 'tink.' It would have been a lucky toss. He was lucky about half the time. He could have looked where he was throwing the empty can but that would have broken the rules. His rules. Another rule required that because he had not heard the 'tink' he would have to open another can while he sat in his driveway.

He had not planned on drinking on the way home from the Food City. He had promised his wife he would not drink while he drove anymore but a promise to her did not change anything. A promise to her was just to shut her up. Besides, a cold beer was how you took the edge off after getting "locked in."

Locking in was what a pilot did once the computer had zeroed in on a target. Locking in did not mean you were going to fire on the target but it did mean that an attack was only a nanosecond away. When you got locked in your focus on the target was complete and nothing else mattered. If the attack was triggered then destroying your enemy was all that mattered. Who else might get hurt, what it would cost, even your own pain were irrelevant concerns once when you were locked in.

He had not been looking for trouble. He was just pulling out of a parking place at the Food City when a punk kid told him, "get your head out of your ass and watch where you're going." It was true, he had not been looking when he backed up and he did come close to hitting the kid's car. "Nobody talks to me like that," he told himself, "At least nobody was going to do it twice. That punk would not do it twice. That's for sure."

He got out of the Mustang and walked over to the punk's car. He walked slowly, taking his time and glancing around the parking lot several times. He was casual and confident, knowing he was being watched, but avoiding looking at the car until he was nearly there.

"What did you say, Shirley?" he said calmly as he leaned into the open window.

He could see the punk sizing him up. As for the kid, he was a stereotype of a wise cracking stoner; long greasy hair, pale skin, pimples, a baggy black tee-shirt with some kind of monster on it, and a cigarette over his left ear.

A nice looking, well groomed younger girl sat on the passenger side of the front seat. Her Food City shirt made him think this was the punk's sister. Clearly she was too classy for the stoner.

There were two good-sized kids in the back seat, but a direct stare at each one insured they would stay where they were.

The punk hesitated, probably concerned about how he looked to his entourage, but a prolonged look at the intensity of the focus in the eyes that were locked in on him made his decision for him.

That was the moment he had been looking for. The moment his target realized his fate. The last slow exhale and the slump of the shoulders as the eyes went blank. He did not really even need the fight itself, the exhilaration came from the victory.

When he saw the humiliation in the punk's eyes he asked again, "Come on Shirley, tell me, what did you say?"

"Nothing," the punk answered softly.

"That's what I thought."

"That's what I thought," he repeated out loud to himself as he sat in his driveway savoring the memory. He finished the third beer, tossed the empty over his shoulder, and waited for the sound.

"Tink."

He laughed. His life could not have been better. Taking the grocery bag under his arm he strolled towards his home. He never saw the person waiting in the shadows by his front door until he felt the arm around his neck. He recognized the sleeper hold but too late to do anything about it. It was a blessing for him to be unconscious as three of his ribs and his upper right leg were broken with what the doctor said was a blunt instrument, probably the baseball bat lying next to him when he was found.

CHAPTER ONE

NATTIE HEARS FROM BOO
(Friday evening)

"Nattie Moreland?" asked a man.

"Yes," Nattie answered. She had a vague recollection of the man's voice and unusual accent, but could not quite place him yet.

"Nattie Moreland the Private Detective?"

"That's me, how can I help you?"

The pitch of the voice went up slightly, "It's me, Beauregard Robinette. You came out to my place in Barton Square a few months ago. Do you remember?"

The trip he was referring to was an investigation into a murder that had taken place in the parking lot of the Never Tell Tavern. Other than the murderer he had been the last person to speak to the victim and additionally he was a witness that placed the victim and Nattie's falsely accused client together just before the murder. Nattie had been fairly convinced that her client was indeed guilty until she interviewed Boo. He had been a counselor in New Orleans before Katrina hit, after which he came to northeast Tennessee to refurbish an old boathouse he inherited from an aunt. Nattie remembered him all right. He was a very large man with long dark thinning hair pulled back in a pony tail, a small gold ring in his left ear, a floral tattoo over his right forearm, and a silk Hawaiian shirt.

"Boo?" she said tentatively hoping she remembered his nickname correctly.

Boo laughed, "You do remember."

"I do. You're the counselor from New Orleans who was refinishing that tavern," confirmed Nattie. "How are you?"

"I could not be doing better. I sold the Never Tell Tavern."

"Well good for you, Boo. You did such a nice job with the interior, it was beautiful. How did the outside turn out?"

"I didn't finish the outside," Boo answered. "Hell! I didn't even start working on it. A woman out of Memphis bought it. She made me an offer I could not refuse."

"So what are you up to now?"

"I'm doing a little cooking and a little bartending while I keep my eyes and ears open for another opportunity."

"Is that why you called? Do you need me to check into an opportunity around Bristol?"

Boo hesitated, "No, that's not why I called. I'm already here in Bristol …"

"Really," she interrupted him, "tell me where you are cooking. I want to come try your red beans and rice. It smelled so good to me that day I came to your place. The man I was with that day, Nathan, raved about it."

"That's real nice Nattie, thank you."

"I mean it," she emphasized, "tell me where you are working. I'll bring my brother, he loves hot food."

Again Boo was quiet for a moment, "Before I tell you where I'm working, let me just tell you why I called."

She realized he had become more serious as his pace slowed and his pitch dropped. "Okay."

"The other night a guy came in and threatened the owner of the bar. The guy is a military type. Lean and mean. Real intense. He really shook up my friend."

Nattie just listened.

"Then last night someone broke his leg while he was getting out of his car."

"Your boss?"

"No, the guy that threatened him. The military guy is the one with the broken leg," he explained. "I want you to find out who did it."

"You want me to find out who broke his leg?"

"I do."

"Aren't the police going to do that?"

5

"Of course, but when they start asking questions they are going to find out that my friend was threatened."

"And that will establish his motive and make him a suspect."

"Exactly."

"Well, I hate to point out the obvious to you, but are you sure he didn't do it?"

"I am. I wasn't with him the whole night but I just know he could not have done it. It isn't in him to do anything like that."

"And you think the only way to prove he didn't do it is to find out who did?"

"That would do it, don't you think?"

"Naturally," agreed Nattie, "but why not just let the police handle it Boo? He'll be a person of interest but they'll figure out that it wasn't him."

"That's not the problem. The problem is that this guy is a real cowboy. He's in the hospital now, but we have to get this solved before he gets healthy because he thinks he has two scores to settle now and that is not going to set well with a guy like him."

"So you want to hire an investigator because you want it solved in a hurry."

"That's right."

"And you thought of me because ... ?"

"Because Frank Lester is Randi Lester's husband."

Nattie remained silent.

Boo explained, "Frank Lester is a helicopter pilot. While he was doing a tour of duty in Iraq, his wife was keeping company with another man."

A knot began forming in Nattie's stomach.

"The man he threatened is my boss, Nathan Moreland, your ex-husband

Nattie heard exactly what she expected to hear, but hearing it still caught her off guard. With her left elbow firmly planted on the desk she cradled her forehead in her hand and wondered, "Why me?"

CHAPTER TWO

NATTIE'S MOM
(Saturday morning)

"Does that look right?" asked Ingrid O'Brien popping a small cube of raw carrot into her mouth. She had diced up one of the five carrots on the cutting board at her end of the kitchen counter.

Looking up from where she was dicing onions on another cutting board at the other end of the counter, Nattie studied her mother. At 55 Ingrid O'Brien was still drawing the attention of young men when she went out. A fitted plaid top and skin-tight blue jeans was her idea of casual at home attire. Ingrid had the same blue eyes, fair skin, light freckles, and sparseness of height as her daughter, but the rich auburn hair and Playboy centerfold body were where they differed.

Why didn't I get your butt? wondered Nattie as she walked past the sink to where her mother stood.

"It looks good to me, Mom. According to Delia you want to cut everything close to the same size so that it all cooks at the same rate."

Delia Davenport was the Food TV celebrity Nattie watched, read, and quoted. Ingrid's skills did not include cooking therefore Nattie's early kitchen education came from her grandmother Vee. Early in her marriage her interest in cooking began when she discovered Delia Davenport. She and Nathan had happened into Zazzy'z Coffee House and Bookstore in Abingdon one afternoon when Delia was there signing copies of her cookbook, Dining With Delia. Nathan bought her an autographed copy of the book which rekindled her interest in cooking, which to that point in their marriage had been limited to heating up soup and microwaving popcorn. It was Delia Davenport's recipe for ribolita soup recipe they were working on.

Ingrid smiled and stroked Nattie's cheek with the back of her fingers, "This is nice. I wish we could do this more often."

"We should."

"Lionel tells me you and Nathan may be getting back together."

Stepping back Nattie sighed. She and her stepfather had never gotten along very well. They were destined to clash, as he was the kind of man who had strong opinions and shared them strongly, and she was the kind of woman who was most comfortable around men who were helpless and dependent. But recently she and he had made some peace when she had solved a case that involved one of the lawyers that worked for him. In a moment of tenderness between them she told him that she was still in love with Nathan.

"That is not exactly what I told him Mom."

A patronizing smile, "What exactly did you tell him then?"

Nattie wiped at her cheek.

"Are you crying?"

"Oh heavens no. It's the onions."

Ingrid eyed her more closely, "Are you sure?"

"Absolutely, mom. It's the onions and I'd like to get it done so I can wash my hands."

Ingrid nodded smugly and let her daughter go back to the onion board.

"I got new business cards," offered Nattie as a way to change the subject.

"That's nice dear."

"Yeah," she continued, "I made my name larger on this card."

No response from Ingrid as she concentrated on making all the carrot pieces of equal size.

"Having to explain that I am not Natasha McMorales is getting old."

Nattie could not tell if her mother was still listening or not. Just like old times.

They worked in silence until Ingrid announced, "I'm done. What's next?"

By this time Nattie was cutting up the kale. Handing her mother three zucchinis, "This is the last of the cutting. Make these half moon slices instead of cubes."

Taking the zucchinis, "Is that what Delia says?"

"It is."

Silence returned to the kitchen for another few minutes while all the chopping was completed. The pace changed when the diced up bacon pieces began cooking in the bottom of the soup pot.

"How long does that have to fry?"

"We're rendering the bacon Mom. And it should take about five minutes."

"Well while the bacon is rendering why don't you show me your new business card."

Nattie retrieved one of her new business cards from her bag hanging over the back of a kitchen chair.

"Very interesting," Ingrid said with enthusiasm as she took the card. "I like the white lettering on the turquoise background."

"Thanks mom, that's Kevin's touch. I wanted turquoise lettering on a white card."

Ingrid lowered the business card and looked her daughter in the eye, "Did he talk you into this design or did he just do it?"

They laughed together. No answer was necessary.

The next step in making the ribolita was to add all the spices, broth, crushed tomatoes, and the vegetables minus the kale and navy beans. This step would take 7 to 10 minutes.

"Let's sit down and talk," Ingrid requested as Nattie adjusted the heat under the soup pot. Taking a mug of coffee she took a seat at the breakfast table.

The phrase made Nattie flinch. The last time Ingrid said 'let's sit down and talk' was the day she told Nattie that her father would not be coming back any more. Nattie's father, Nathan Johnson was a functional alcoholic during most of her childhood but just before she hit puberty, a critical time for girls and their fathers, he had an accident that cost a little girl her life. His drinking got worse after that and eventually cost him his job and then his family. The phrase did not remind her of a banner day in her life.

After refilling her coffee cup Nattie took the seat across the breakfast table from her mother, "So, what's the good news?"

"No news, I just wanted to talk." Noticing the suspicious expression on Nattie's face, "Don't give me that look Natalie. I swear, can't a mother just have an innocent conversation with her adult daughter without it meaning something bad?"

"Of course a mom can do that. Is that what you're doing?"

"Okay, okay! I have an agenda. Sue me. I'm just worried about you. Does that make me a bad mother?"

"That depends on what you are worried about and what you do about it."

"I'm worried about your future."

"What about my future, mother?"

Placing the Natasha McMorales Detective Agency business card on the table, "I know you are having fun with this now, but please honey, what kind of life will it be like in ten years? Or twenty years?"

Nattie's eyes rolled involuntarily.

"Seriously, what do you picture it will be like when you turn fifty?"

Grinning, "I was rather hoping to grow into a fifty year old body like yours."

Ingrid sat back and took a sip from her coffee mug.

That shut you up, thought Nattie savoring the victory. Verbal duels with her mother usually left her in knots.

Gazing at her mug as she held it with both hands Ingrid turned the tables with her somber tone, "I'm being serious. I don't see how you are ever going to meet anyone while you are in that profession."

"By 'anyone' do you mean an eligible man?"

"You know exactly what I mean. What's wrong with wanting someone to settle down with or to grow old with?"

Nattie could feel the muscles on the back of her neck tightening, "There is absolutely nothing wrong with that, mother, as long as it is the right person."

Putting her mug down Ingrid reached across the table and squeezed Nattie's hand. Using her victim tone of voice she added, "I just want you to be happy."

With her hand on top of her mother's hand, "I am happy mother."

"I know you are. But what about companionship?"

"If it happens it happens. If it doesn't it doesn't. I don't see any value in worrying about it."

Shifting to her teacher voice Ingrid withdrew her hand. Sitting back, "I just don't want you to worry."

"What do you want, mother? Should I quit my job? Go back to school? Put an ad in the paper?"

Shifting her tone of voice once again, "Of course that's what I want; quit your job, put an ad in the paper, and go back to school. I hear belly dancers are making a comeback."

Wow, sarcasm, that's something new in your bag of tricks.

"Can you just answer one question for me?"

"Yes mother, what is it?"

Standing up she placed a hand on Nattie's shoulder, "Are you still in love with Nathan?"

Their eyes locked for a long moment, "Yes."

Squeezing Nattie's shoulder, "Then please honey, don't just take the 'if it happens it happens' attitude. If you want him, take him, you know he's yours." A smile and another squeeze of the shoulder marked the end of the conversation. "I'm going to the little girl's room."

Loving him and wanting him are not the same thing. It takes a lot more than that to make a marriage work, lamented Nattie.

While her mother was otherwise occupied Nattie took a bottle of Shiraz from her backpack and poured four glugs into the soup pot. Before marrying Lionel Ingrid would not have thought twice about cooking with wine but Lionel did not allow alcohol in the house so Nattie had to improvise. The recipe called for a cup of wine and according to Delia a glug was approximately a quarter cup.

Nattie had the wine stowed away before her mother returned. "My turn, and then I have to go." I have to go and then I have to go, passed through her thoughts, which led her to the next thought, oh great, now I'm thinking like Kevin.

"Do you have an appointment?" asked Ingrid as she walked arm in arm to the front door with Nattie.

"I do. It's a case that I haven't decided I'm going to take."

"What about lunch?"

"I'll grab a bite where I'm going."

"Where is that?"

"Why the questions mom?" She looked more closely at her mother, "You already know where I'm going don't you mom?"

Ingrid tried unsuccessfully to fight off her smug smile.

Pointing an accusatory finger, "Kevin told you I'm having lunch at Nathan's place." I'll kill him.

"As long as you are there you might as well make the most of it."

"Look mom, I appreciate your concern, I really do, but things with Nathan are complicated."

Placing her hands on Nattie's shoulders she asked, "Too complicated for Natasha McMoreland? I don't think so. You, my darling daughter," kissing Nattie's forehead lightly, "can do whatever you put your mind to."

Nattie noticed that her mother had mispronounced McMorales but let it go, "Thanks mom. You do okay for yourself too."

Ingrid smiled and whispered, "I'll let you in on a secret. While you were in the bathroom I put a cup of Merlot in the soup."

CHAPTER THREE

NATTIE CONFRONTS NATHAN
(Saturday early afternoon)

Nattie lunged for her water glass. She had eaten the Our House chili before. Our House, Nathan's tavern, was known for two things; every hour on the hour the patrons would sing "Our House" by Crosby, Stills, and Nash, and a menu that featured several variations of hamburger, all loaded and all cheap. Chili was usually the healthiest thing on the menu, but this was not the same chili. This chili was flaming hot.

"What did you do to the chili?"

"What do you mean?" Nathan asked in an innocent disposition that had never fooled her when they were married. It was certainly not going to fool her now.

Gulping down half a beer stein of water Nattie ignored his question. "Boo?" she asked.

"Boo," he answered, shaking his head in agreement. "Do you like it?"

She looked at the bowl on the bar in front of her, "Well, it should increase your beer sales."

"Do you want a beer then?"

"No thanks, but I am going to need more crackers."

"Crackers are free," he complained.

"Not my fault."

Nathan smiled and then reached under the bar to retrieve a basket full of saltine cracker packets. "Anything else?" he asked leaning forward to watch her crumble several crackers into her chili.

She held up a finger as she took another small spoon full.

"Better?" he asked while her mouth was still full.

"Much," she said after swallowing. "It also helps that I was prepared for it this time."

"Maybe I should put a warning label on the bowl. I don't want anyone to get hurt in here."

"It's funny you should mention people getting hurt Nathan."

She had waited for a natural time to broach the subject of Frank Lester and had been very careful to use a conversational tone but the effort was to no avail. Nathan, ever vigilant to her disapproval stiffened immediately and stepped back.

"What?" he asked in a lower voice.

"We need to talk about that guy who threatened you last week."

Squinting and shuffling back and forth he attempted to minimize the event. "It was no big deal Nattie, really. It was just a misunderstanding. Nothing more."

Raising an eyebrow, "And yet, shortly after threatening you he was attacked in his own driveway."

He leaned back against the bar and relaxed his shoulders again, "Do you really think that was me? Come on, Nattie, can you picture me doing something like that?"

"No. I don't think you did it, Nathan."

Straightening up he grinned, "You see, no problem."

"The problem, Nate, is that you are a person of interest."

"But you know I didn't do it."

She leaned closer, "I know you couldn't have done it but the police don't know you like I do."

Nathan bowed his head as he ran his index finger lightly over the back of Nattie's hand, "No one knows me like you do, Nattie."

Nattie sat and watched him stroke the back of her hand for several moments before slowly raising her head and matter-of-factly asking, "Does Randi Lester **know** you Nathan?"

The question startled him enough that he quickly jerked his head back. Nattie regretted the harshness of her question as she listened to his barely audible gasp for breath.

"I told you I was seeing someone months ago Nattie. Don't you remember when we drove back from that tavern out in Barton Square? You went there to interview that bartender, remember?"

His tentative eye contact and nervous glances reminded her of a hamster. She watched him silently.

"I know," he confessed in a lower voice. "I didn't mention that she was married." Spreading his arms, "Can you blame me?"

To this question she added a raised eyebrow to her silence.

Blushing, "I guess that was a silly question. Blaming your ex-husband is the national pastime for ex-wives."

Ex-wives with nothing better to do maybe, thought Nattie as she reassured him, "Look Nathan, I am not here to blame you, but I am going to need to talk to you about her."

"I don't see why," he stated curtly. "It was just a fling. Someone to spend some time with and that's about all it was. And now it's over so case closed."

Eyeing him through narrowing eyelids, "And yet her husband came here and threatened you."

He took his turn to be silent.

"Did your relationship with her end before or after he threatened you?"

"Before," he stated indignantly. "It isn't really any of your business though is it? It's not like I'm your client."

"No, I am," came the deep resounding voice of Boo Robinette. Neither had noticed him approaching.

Nathan turned and pointed at the big man, "You are?" [pause] "You are what? Her client?"

Boo nodded, "I hired her. She's going to find out who really took a baseball bat to that guy who came in here to threatened you."

Nathan looked confused, "That was before you started working here, wasn't it?"

"I was here that night," Boo remembered, "I sat right there where she is now."

Nathan snapped his fingers, "You were drinking Southern Comfort and tonic."

Boo nodded his agreement.

15

Leaning on the bar with his left elbow and with his back to Nattie Nathan effectively cut her out of the conversation, "Why do you think I need a detective? According to the police I'm just a, a, ... what did they call it?"

"A person of interest," offered Nattie over his shoulder.

Stepping back to once again include her, "And that's not so bad, right Nattie?"

Tipping her head to the right she said, "It's not much evidence, but still, people have been convicted on pretty shaky evidence in the past."

"I'm not concerned about the police. I doubt they really think you did it anyway," explained Boo. "I'm worried about that nut-job. Until we figure out who really did it he's going to blame you and that means he is going to be coming back. Somewhere sometime he is going to be evening the score. I could see it in his eyes."

Flipping his hand over Nathan dismissed Boo's concern, "He's not coming back. He doesn't care about her that much."

"That doesn't matter to guys like him."

"What does matter to guys like him, Boo?" asked Nattie in a teacher-like tone that told Nathan the question was for his benefit.

Addressing Nattie but speaking to Nate Boo explained, "To him, Nate here took something that belongs to him. It doesn't matter if he wants her or not. To him, she is a belonging and Nate is a thief. Scaring Nate might have been enough for him then, but that was before someone broke his leg with a baseball bat." Then turning to face Nate squarely he added, "He is not going to let that go."

"Which means he now thinks he has two scores to settle with you," added Nattie.

Nathan glared at her but said nothing. There was nothing to say. She was right about this. She knew things about he and Randi that he did not want her to know and she was right about that too. She was always right and he resented her for it. *Why can't she just be a little bit more human?* he wondered for the umpteenth time.

"Okay," he said turning towards Boo Robinette, "I agree I need help. But why her?"

Yeah, she thought, *why me?*

Check out other titles at

csthompsonbooks.com

*AUTHOR'S BLOG

*PHOTOS

*AUTHOR'S BIO

*EXCERPTS OF FUTURE BOOKS

*SHORT VIDEOS OF AUTHOR READING

*MUSIC OF THE MONTH